MAXIM JAKUBOWSKI
is a former publisher who founded and still
owns London's Murder One bookshop. As
well as being a writer and editor of various
cult publishing imprints, he is
acknowledged as a disturbing and
controversial voice in contemporary fiction.
His collections have sold massively, he is a
regular on TV and radio where he is an
expert on crime, erotica and film, and a
Guardian columnist. *On Tenderness
Express* is his first novel in the Private Eye
genre.

First Published in Great Britain in 2000 by
The Do-Not Press Limited
16 The Woodlands
London SE13 6TY

C-format paperback: ISBN 1 899344 54 3
Casebound edition: ISBN 1 899 344 55 1
Limited edition casebound: ISBN 1899 344 56 X

British Library Cataloguing in Publication Data. A catalogue
record for this book is available from the British Library.

h g f e d c b a

Printed and bound in Great Britain by
The Guernsey Press Co Ltd.

On Tenderness
Express

Maxim Jakubowski

Fiction by Maxim Jakubowski

Life in the World of Women*
It's You That I Want to Kiss*
Because She Thought She Loved Me*
The State of Montana*
The Phosphorus War

(*published by The Do-Not Press)

"For in tremendous extremities,
human souls are like drowning men; well enough
they know they are in peril, well enough
they know the causes of that peril,
nonetheless, the sea is the sea, and these
drowning men do drown."

Herman Melville

....

For Dolores

DRAGGING AROUND THE CHAINS OF LOVE

1: Martin

I am a liar.

An unconvincing narrator. A most unreliable witness.

So feel free to believe or not whatever I say. You may judge me for all I care, decree that I am guilty of this or that, or blameless, or indifferent.

Your call.

As for me, I don't give a fuck.

So, how did it all begin?

Barely a year ago.

In London.

A suite of offices in Holborn in a massive building of grey stone. Traffic gridlocked outside the bay windows of the suite, the sheer greyness of a British autumn morning already leaking into the soul and bodies of all of us. Joan, my assistant cum secretary cum decorative addition to the IKEA decor of the offices I was renting was away ill, yet again suffering from migraine. I was bored, idly surfing the Internet on my laptop, joining chat rooms left right and centre, spreading doubt and equivocation as I adopted a new persona on each occasion, swapping cybergender, teasing, provoking, offering myself, playing coy, alternately knowing or falsely innocent. As good a way to waste time as any other.

I was forty-four.

At forty-four, F. Scott Fitzgerald of St Louis, Minnesota, had already drunk himself to death. No such luck for me. I couldn't even stand the taste of alcohol and if anything was going to kill me in the long term, it was the subtle blend of caffeine and sugar in the Coke or Pepsi which I drank by the gallon. An ambiguous death wish if ever there was one. How could death by cola ever be romantic?

I had money in the bank and no will to live.

Sitting there, morose, waiting for the past to catch up.

Counting the pulses of the cursor on the computer screen, as it metronomically awaited my further orders to set sail for another forum.

Or the welcome interruption of a telephone call.

But all I had for company was the pain deep inside.

Until the knock on the door.

Business. The best possible distraction.

He was tall and beefy and boringly dressed in a brown double-breasted suit, hair trimmed regulation office length, early signs of baldness already visible, mid-thirties I reckoned. Corporate type. Small squinting eyes, thin colourless eyebrows, grey socks peering between trouser turn ups and sensible City shoes. Wife having an affair was my first guess. I handed him my card ' Martin Jackson, Private Investigations. Nothing Gained. Just the facts in exchange for your treasured cash. Nothing too Sordid, please'. He flinched. Just another geezer with no sense of humour.

I asked him to sit down.

A police siren faded in and out from the busy street outside. He coughed.

He took out a cigarette. Remembered distractedly to offer me the pack. I declined.

'You come highly recommended,' he said.

'That's nice to know,' I answered, not in the least bothered who had given him my name. By hook or by crook, I do my jobs and then draw a final line under them when they are completed. 'So…?'

He squirmed in his chair, throwing me insecure glances across the desk.

'Naturally, anything you say is in utter confidence,' I tried to reassure him. 'Even if we agree not to pursue the matter further.'

He nodded.

Then raised his receding chin an inch or so and spat it out. 'It's my wife.'

Bingo.

It usually is.

The look on my own face remained impassive. The few friends I used to have always said I should play poker. Hadn't done since my teens when matchsticks were the only stakes.

'Your wife?' Sympathetically.

'Yes.'

'And?'

It was the usual story, with some variations. There are no new stories.

Couple marry. Probably too young. Go through poor but happy days together, hand in hand, hearts oblivious of deeper realities. Careers begin (his, at least). Money worries. The inevitable cooling down of ardour. Neglect. Wanderlust. Pressures accumulate. A fraught house move and mortgage complications. She feels he is now taking her for granted. He can feel her becoming distant. Both increasingly working late, only greeting each other quietly as they undress for bed at night. Their lovemaking is dull and predictable. One day, her face looks different, there is a shiny otherness present; she is dreamier than ever. Strangely distant. Indifferent. He suspects another man but dares not ask. Then, one day, a letter arrives in his in-tray at work. Accusing her, denouncing her extra-marital activities. He can stand it no longer and confronts her. At first, in tears, she denies it but soon breaks down and admits to the affair. Promises him she will end it immediately. Blames him partly for his unthinkable blindness all these past months. He swears he will forgive her. They will start again.

Spend more time together. It all ends in tears, in each other's arms at three in the morning. Feeling closer together than ever, or at any rate, since their initial coming together as students in Cambridge and the no frills wedding in the college chapel. So, it's all decided, the marriage will endure. Her affair will deliberately be forgotten. Erased in his memory. But two days later she doesn't return in the evening from work. He assumes she's missed her customary 6.27 commuter train. He goes to the station to meet the next one. He'd returned earlier to prepare dinner himself. A simple vegetable salad. He's vegetarian. She isn't on the following train. Or the one after. He haunts the station until the final train comes and goes, rushing between the station and their new house to check on telephone messages. There are none. The following day he phones her job and discovers she had taken the previous day off. Another day goes by and he forces himself to go to work, his heart seizing every time the phone rings. But it never is his wife. He assumes the worst. That she might have gone back to her lover and will never return to him. During their initial row, in a spirit of appeasement, he had carefully refrained from asking the man's identity. He now bitterly regrets this. He hasn't a clue who her lover might be. Never had a clue while it was going on; doesn't have a clue now.

It's been nearly three weeks now. He's past the heartbreak. Just worried. Not a word from her, she hasn't even returned home to retrieve her clothes, her books and other personal things. So unlike her. He hasn't changed the locks, assuming she would have come visit during the daytime while he was at work to retrieve her belongings. No one has heard from her at her publishing office. They're angry. None of this makes sense to him.

So, now, he's sitting in my office, the latest in a long line of unhappy husbands. Pale demeanour, sorry eyes, shaving cuts dotting his square chin. Isn't my job great!

'Have you been in touch with the police?' I asked my hapless visitor.

He hadn't. Still felt she would somehow return to the harbour of his arms; after all, they had made up, or so he felt. He had forgiven her, and it would be too embarrassing to place the whole matter in the public domain. So his brother, an architect in South London, had suggested using a detective. Just to find out the truth. And if she had left him for good for the other man, at least there would be confirmation. A sense of closure.

'Yes, closure is very important,' I said.

He nodded.

For once, we were on the same wave-length.

'So,' he finally asked. 'Can you take the…' he hesitated to use the word 'case'; too many bad films and books had depreciated the word. 'Are you willing to look into this?'

I agreed to. A job is a job after all.

I explained the leads I would pursue, the time involved, the effort, the likely cost. Cheque or cash would be fine, I preferred not to take credit cards.

He passed over the envelope he had brought along, containing an assortment of photographs of his wife taken over past years (one taken in sand dunes outside of Scarborough on the Yorkshire coast, another with her tousled hair windswept in front of the Beaubourg Centre in Paris on an autumn day the previous year, he pointed out), addresses: where she worked, the friends he knew she had. I asked further questions, desultory queries about her life before him, parents, university, likes and dislikes. I studiously noted down the answers on my pad, feigning interest and attention.

'I'll do my best,' I reassured him as I led him to the door. He left.

I made an immediate beeline for the toilet and was violently sick.

Two hours later, I felt no better. The nausea still treated my whole body as occupied territory, and as much as I tried to exert some will power, there was not even a hint of a resistance army regrouping, ready to fight the drop dead feeling that appeared to have won the war within. I still wanted to vomit, but there was just bile lurking inside me and that only made things worse. I locked up and walked the hundred yards to the first of the legion of sandwich shops in the nearby area. Egg, cress and mayonnaise on white bread. Yes, once inside me that sort of lethal formula should do the trick. Help me be sick again as the vile mixture curdled in my throat and stomach. But somehow the food settled and all I was left with was a feeling of utter emptiness.

On my desk, the brown envelope Christopher Streetfield had left lay unopened. I toyed with it, tracing its shape, weighing it in the palm of my hand, holding it to the light. Photographs, a list of names and numbers. What was left of a man's life after the fall of the bomb of lust...

A sorry landscape.

Inside my head, it felt like a pressure cooker.

I desperately needed something to happen.

It did.

At this stage in a *noir* book or movie, a husky-voiced long-haired blonde knocks on the door and asks the private eye to search for her missing friend or relative, with ambiguous hints of payment in bodily kind thrown in.

She didn't even knock. She walked straight in.

Her hair was auburn, though, and cut short.

And it was her younger sister she sought. A little sister, with ironic shades of Chandler! I was sure I'd read the book already. But it hadn't involved John Le Carré the first time around.

She'd found me, of all places, in the Yellow Pages. I didn't even know I was there. Kept on being rude over the phone to tele-salesmen trying to convince me of its display virtues. Strange how fate plays little tricks on you.

Her name was Nola Poshard. French grandparents, and I suspected some far back miscegenation in the family, a hint of darkness in her skin and eyes, some exotic, venomous flower, predatory, cold-hearted but siren-like attractive. Nola.

The sister's name was Louise.

Nola had come into possession of a major book collection. A past lover of Nola's had left it to her some years previously, to assuage his guilt or hers over previous indiscretions or heartbreak. She had kept the bulky collection, of mostly modern firsts, in storage for ages, having no particular interest in its contents or what the books had represented for her erstwhile lover. I got the impression he might even have killed himself over her, but the hard expression on her face when she related the collection's history prevented me from inquiring further.

Eventually, she had decided the cumbersome collection needed valuing and had been amazed by the final figure the rare book dealer had quoted her. He had also recommended that, should she wish to realise its maximum value, it would be preferable to sell in separate lots, or at any rate some of the best pieces individually. One item in particular had intrigued him. A seemingly one-of-a-kind curio. A book he'd actually heard of but which he had always suspected was apocryphal. Not actually a book, as she explained, but an advance uncorrected bound proof.

Le Carré, having completed his new novel, *The Night Manager*, had his secretary send his publishers the diskette. This was eagerly welcomed and passed on to the production department so that advance proofs might be printed for major buyers, reviewers and other publicity and marketing purposes. On receipt of these, several copies were biked to the author's Hampstead house where it was soon discovered, to utter dismay, that the diskette in question had been that of the first draft and not his final version of the novel. Further, the initial draft actually named many of the real names of persons and companies involved in the Arms for Iraq controversy which had partly inspired the novelist. All the proofs were summarily destroyed and the process repeated with the correct diskette. Though not end of story, as Le Carré's publishers were then already in the process of takeover talks with a smaller, more aggressive house. Maybe someone in production or dispatch or any department threatened by future cuts had managed to secrete a copy of the proof's first stage before they had all been pulped? Allegedly, according to the dealer, one copy had once surfaced at an auction in Texas, but this was unconfirmed.

Seeing the volume amongst the cardboard boxes temporarily housing Nola Poshard's inherited collection, he had remembered the tale and distractedly checked the final chapter of the book (both the first and the second proofs sported the same cover). And, there it was, a different ending to the one he remembered. It was difficult to actually ascribe a value to this one-off, but he was confident that it would fetch a premium price amongst American collectors due to its unique nature and the curious publishing history that surrounded it.

'So,' I asked Nola Poshard. 'What happened to the book then?'

'The proof,' she corrected me.

'What happened to the proof?'

'The little slut stole it,' she said.

'Tell me about her, your younger sister.'

'What do you want to know?'

'Basically everything,' I answered. 'If I am to find her, those sort of details do come in handy...'

Louise wasn't actually her sister, but a half-sister. A fish-out-of-water blonde in a family whose antecedents stretched back to early Cajun days in New Orleans, and where fiery hair and darker skin were the norm. I was thankfully spared centuries of family history, and given the bare bones. From the tone of Nola's voice, Louise certainly sounded like the black sheep of the family, but then I had the feeling Nola was herself no stranger to black thoughts or actions and this was a bad case of pot and kettle. But a potential client is a client and you just keep your trap shut if you wish to stay in the private eye business.

I completed my note-taking and began my usual spiel about expenses, costs and this and that and confidentiality and ethics, But Nola quickly interrupted me.

'Yeah, I know all that, Mr Jackson. So spare me the details. I can afford you and the time it takes to track down the little bitch. All I want to know is whether you can take the case on or not.'

'I can,' I answered.

'And right now?' she queried me, her gaze landing on Streetfield's brown envelope on my desk. 'Do you have any other cases on at present?'

'No. I'm quite free to take your assignment, Ms Poshard,' I replied with great assurance. 'Nothing else in progress.'

'Good,' a thin smile crossed her scarlet lips. 'Because I want you to devote one hundred percent of your time in finding Louise, and the book of course. You should have no distractions.'

'In all fairness,' I pointed out, 'the cost of the operation could well mount up to much more than the value of the book, you know.'

'I'm aware of that, Mr Jackson, but that's beside the point.'

'If you say so, Ms Poshard,' I noted.

'I do.'

'And when I catch up with Louise, do you want me to get the Le Carré proof back for you? Or just advise you of its whereabouts and hers?'

'Find her first. I will then decide on the next step to be taken,' she said.

Something gave me the feeling that she didn't give a damn for the book, however rare it might happen to be. It was her little half-sister Louise she wanted back. And badly.

We got down to business. I had a long list of questions. I opened my notebook again.

Nola Poshard didn't have all the answers and it was agreed I would visit her house the following day for the photographs and documents and extra information I required to tackle the case properly. I also wanted to see Louise's erstwhile room there. How often people left simple clues behind when they did a disappearing trick. Although not seemingly Mrs Streetfield... My new employer paid the upfront money in crisp bank notes, that still smelled of the deep corruption of a bank vault as opposed to the shabby filth of the corner cash dispenser.

I watched her as she rose and made her way to the door. A classic backside and legs to kill for. Stockings for sure.

'Until tomorrow, Mr Jackson,' she said, peering briefly over her shoulders.

'I will have made some enquiries already by the time we see each other,' I assured her, my eyes still fixed on the horizon of her panty-line, daydreaming of the tanned flesh and its treasures barely concealed by the taut material of her black skirt.

'That would be nice,' Nola Poshard murmured as she walked out the door. Echoing my thoughts exactly.

Once again I was on my own. With the muted, almost distant

sounds of the Holborn afternoon traffic for company. The Streetfield envelope and its contents sat silently on the desk as if in a spotlight. The knot in my throat tightened. I took the brown package and buried it inside the left drawer. Next to my passport, post office savings book and last will and testament. Forced my mind to travel back to the swishing noise the stockinged thighs of Nola Poshard made as she sashayed out of the office earlier, her smell all animal, radiating lust with natural allure. Yes, she was damn attractive, that I knew. But there was also danger there. Essence of femme fatale. Just like in a book.

That's how it all began.

Two cases. Two women.

The second and final part of the story of my fall.

2: Cornelia

There were few things Cornelia cared about.

The dance, the music and her books.

She knew she didn't fit in, hadn't emerged from the same mould as other women.

Or men.

But basically, she didn't give a damn.

She was self-sufficient, had no starry ambitions, lived for the moment and knew that if worse came to worse she would always somehow survive.

Because she had the moves. And she had the looks.

There again, her looks didn't conform with fashion or boring standards of beauty, but they were distinctive and she knew from past experience that they worked; she could turn on the charm at will. Bed most men or women she set her eyes on.

And, within limits, she also enjoyed sex.

Although, whenever she found leisure time enough to reflect on the matter, she also found the occupation highly overrated. Entertaining, yes, but the pleasures it provided her were as much mental as they were sensual and body-related.

Cornelia had no heart.

She couldn't blame the fact on a poor childhood or traumas of the past or any other plausible excuse. She'd been born into a relaxed middle-class environment, her parents had never divorced (despite a parade of explosive rows over the years which she often witnessed with much puzzlement but little anguish), she'd never lacked for anything, so she reckoned she just must have been born that way.

She couldn't understand this thing called 'love'.

It just escaped her.

And neither could she stand the sight of pets.

So, by the age of twenty-five she had accumulated a baker's dozen of past lovers in her smooth passage through teenage years and early adulthood, none of them having ever graduated to live-in status for more than a couple of weeks; been the object of three requests for marriage and been on the wrong side of two failed suicide attempts which both men blamed on her cold, indifferent heart; had enjoyed a brilliant academic career and attained a supreme form of confidence that convinced her she would continue sailing through life with much ease, but needed some sort of hobby to keep the boredom at bay.

On the rare occasion she confided with her mother about her lack of empathy with other members of the species and the fact that few subjects managed to grip her attention long enough to exercise her imagination, her mother was reminded of a charming anecdote which, although rather funny at the time, now contained the paradox of Cornelia's life in a nutshell. As a child, Cornelia would always tire of new toys and dolls within hours and would sit around moping on the carpet, and when asked what the matter was – she had only begun to speak a few weeks before – answered that she was boring; what she had tried to say was that she was bored.

She was capable of demonstrations of affection, so that could pass muster, she reckoned. So, it was just a matter of pretending. In both high school and then Yale, she involved herself heavily in student theatrics; she had the perfect looks and distance to play most ingenues in the repertoire, and sci-entifically used this training in her trajectory through the world of men and lust and other distractions.

When the time came for her to choose a subject for her

thesis, she was at a loss for ideas. Most of the angles academia suggested did not attract her in the slightest. To everyone's surprise, not least her somewhat shocked and bemused tutors, she opted for sociology and an in-depth study of the sex business in the Boston area, suggested by some copy-editing she had done for student publications and then a small magazine devoted to literary erotica started by two budding ex-student entrepreneurs she had worked with on the student journals.

For a whole year, she immersed herself in the seamy side of Massachusetts life, frequenting topless bars, interviewing strippers and local whores, gaining access to hidden away brothels which catered for both the student and business pop-ulation of the area. Her subject was frowned upon by the university and there were threats to withdraw her research grant and not a little controversy on the campus. But she was clearly fascinated by the subject and one of the most gifted students in her year, and a little pressure she covertly exerted through a journalist she had somewhat conveniently bedded soon saw the academic authorities come to their senses and accept her work.

She was granted a PhD with honours.

Her approach to her subject had proven impeccably detached, intellectually rigorous and defused any sordid aspects her trawl through the the world of sex as a commer-cial transaction might have raised.

So Cornelia was now Cornelia PhD.

And at a dead end.

The conquest of academia had effortlessly been accom-plished and the concept of further challenges to overcome held little attraction. Of course, she knew she now had to make a living. Her parents were willing to help out for a short period if necessary, but Cornelia knew she had to survive on her own, with no obligations to others holding her back.

At this stage, she knew only one thing: she had no wish to ever become an academic and follow the career path she had borrowed until now. The people and atmosphere just bored her.

She found a junior editorial position with a minor New York publishing house and moved to the West Village where she found a small apartment she could barely afford. After just three months, life bored her again and, further, she was flat broke. Because by now she had an expensive habit. Not drugs; she'd tried some, they did nothing for her. Books. She'd always found, from childhood onward, that reading was the best cure for boredom and had quickly begun accumulating a collection of her favourite books. At Yale, in the countless used books emporiums that still littered the Boston suburbs, she had come across countless first editions of books she had particularly enjoyed and began collecting certain authors, genres or illustrators. The walls of her studio were carpeted with wooden shelves groaning under the weight of her books, every one carefully shielded in protective plastic covers which she would finger with the nearest she would ever come to love. Her books became her life. She moved from the publishing house to a magazine company who were willing to pay her an extra five thousand dollars per year, even if the job mainly consisted in penning more literate blurbs to accompany the fuzzy photographs of celebrities in various states of undress supplied by the paparazzi of the world or snatched from video screens and movies the actors would have wished to erase once and forever from their filmography.

But as her book collecting progressed – by now, Cornelia had moved from provincial used bookstores and thrift shops to the Strand's rare book room and dealer's catalogues – so did the prices she was having to pay for her discoveries.

A genuine first edition of John Irving's *A Son of the Circus* came her way and she sadly found she couldn't afford it. Her pride precluded assistance from her parents or reliance on a loan. Cornelia realised she had to find new ways to make money. She convinced the dealer in Bethesda to hold the volume for her for a week until she had puzzled out her financial predicament.

A chance encounter outside the St Mark's Bookshop the following day offered an unexpected solution.

'Hey, Cornelia,' a woman's voice shouted out.

Cornelia looked up and recognised a woman she had interviewed two years before in Boston, when she was researching her thesis. She couldn't recall her name. They had a drink together and one hour later Cornelia auditioned for a bar in Alphabet City which was short of strippers. She knew she had a body and looks men lusted for. She was no prude. It just sounded like easy money to supplement her publishing wages.

In retrospect, she knew her audition must have proven somewhat amateurish. She'd tried to recall all the bump and grind moves she had observed in such a detached manner previously, but found she couldn't attain the same level of vulgarity. She would have to find her own moves, her own style. She knew she was too stiff and could see from the puzzled look on his face that the joint's booker (or was he the owner?) couldn't quite make her out. She stood butt-naked in front of him, the bar was empty, her grey CK underwear crumpled on the ground where she had thrown it in the throes of her stumbling dance. She moved up to him. Unzipped him and sucked him off. The whole procedure only took a few wordless minutes. He came inside her mouth. She detached herself from the bar-owner's cock, took a few steps back, grasped a glass from the counter and spat out his come.

'When can I start?' Cornelia asked.

One week later, the John Irving first was on her shelf.

Four weeks later, she left her publishing job. She could

earn as much money doing six shifts a week stripping. She found another, better quality club, where the men tipped better and made less demands, which allowed her to concentrate on her dancing and develop her particular style. As befits a Yale PhD, Cornelia felt she could make her own rules, and made it a rule to restrict her sex work to dance alone; no shower work, mud or fat wrestling or private sessions behind closed doors. And she charged twice as much as the other women for a lap dance, which only served to make her more desirable to the men who could afford her.

It was just work, she reasoned. Her body was a commodity and she was not selling it, just supplying it on loan. It allowed her more leisure time to read, see movies, relax. Initially, the new life was good.

But book collecting is just another vice. It feeds on itself and never stops. Every new book acquired breeds interest or need in another, often more elusive as well as expensive.

The prices dealers or catalogues were quoting began to soar.

Cornelia ruled out prostitution, or running like a mad cow between too many clubs and bars in search of the extra necessary greenbacks, as a step too far, and began making enquiries into ways of making quick money when the right book came onto the market.

She had the looks and the intelligence, and her questions in the dressing rooms and dark bars soon found the right ear.

There was a phone call, followed by a meeting she had to attend blindfolded.

The man in the darkness facing her had asked her if she knew how to handle a gun.

She had. Her father had taught her and she had been on the university shooting team, it had been a momentary challenge.

A proposal was made to her.

Someone out there recognised her quirky talents and thought she was made of the right stuff.

No harm would come to her if she said no.

And the money was excellent.

She was given a week to come to a decision.

It only took Cornelia forty-eight hours to make her mind up.

It was just another transaction. She needed the money; someone needed a job done.

She wasn't even nervous about this new and decisive turn in her life. She knew her affection for other people bordered on the non-existent and that she didn't suffer from guilt. Neither was she religious or sentimental. Or even squeamish (apart from snakes or eels or other such slithering beasts).

So, it was agreed.

There would be telephone calls and there would be occasional jobs.

The assignments would be infrequent and she was given latitude to turn any down so it wouldn't be counted against her. A few months down the line, she asked for the arrangements to be changed, so that she would just make contact and indicate her willingness to take on a job. That is, each time a new book came on the market which she could ill afford to purchase from the proceeds of her dancing.

He – or was it they? – at any rate, it was always the same voice at the other end of the phone line, readily agreed to this.

Thus did Cornelia Irish's new life begin.

Exotic dancer, as some still described her chosen profession, book collector and killer.

She would always remember the first book she killed for. It became a prized item on her shelves. A symbol of her independence from the nine to five grind. Two thousand dollars it had cost her. A copy of the much sought-after Doubleday edition of J.G. Ballard's *The Atrocity Exhibition*. Most of the initial print-run had been pulped and publication cancelled. Few volumes had survived and he was an author she liked, even though this particular book was her least favourite. Too linear; Cornelia loved the art of the story where a tale went from A to B. She'd always been somewhat systematic in her approach to life, always taking new steps in her stride, climbing every mountain or molehill in turn, one at a time, with downright obstinacy in her refusal to panic, whatever the circumstances.

The doorman cum bouncer at her club had put her in touch with the Organisation. They had arranged for her to pick up the gun in the cabin of a peep show close to Forty-second Street before the onset of Disneyfication. An East German small calibre. The hit was a name called Vargas, a South American businessman. A pencil-thin guy in his thirties. She'd met up with him at the bar of the Royalton on East Forty-fourth Street. He thought she was a high-priced whore and Cornelia did nothing to change his opinion. It had been a few months since she'd last had sex with a man and this one was not unattractive. One on one in his hotel room, she felt, was a safer option and, after all, she needed a fuck, and sending him on his way with a satisfied libido would do no harm. He was still dozing in bed as she put the cushion over his head and pulled the trigger. The gun had a silencer. No mess, clean kill. She felt quite proud of herself. She had already dressed and was out of the room five minutes later, having carefully cleaned all the surfaces she remembered having touched while Vargas fingered and caressed her. Extra precaution: she even took the soggy condom from the bin and disposed of it a few blocks away. She wasn't sure whether police scientists could get a DNA trace from her own secretions on the outside of the latex, but there was no point taking unnecessary risks.

So easy.

And she bought the Ballard book and had cash to spare.

There were two more hits in the following six months. The Egyptian businessman also wanted to bed her, but that night Cornelia wasn't in the mood and anyway the guy had greasy fingers and made her shiver every time he touched her. She excused herself and visited the bathroom. Took the gun from her purse and unlocked the safety. When she emerged from the bathroom, the short, fat guy was already half undressed, standing there by the elaborate four-poster bed of the Broadway luxury hotel, his bulging stomach straining against a white vest that barely reached his navel, his cock still soft, and still wearing grey socks held up by suspenders. The sight of the socks and the suspenders was even more ridiculous than his cock still at half-mast and his broad smile as he saw her move closer to him.

'I thought you had gone in there to undress, my dear,' he said. Then noticed the gun in her hand, aimed at his heart.

But Cornelia had the advantage of surprise. Overweight men in a state of undress and still wearing socks don't tend to react very fast.

She quickly raised the gun and shot him through his forehead. Out of the corner of her eye, she caught sight of some bone and brain matter and a corolla of blood whistling through the air in slow motion behind him, like fireworks against the room's cream-coloured walls. The unholy mess landed on the bed before the Arab's body finally hit the floor. Back in the corridor, she was about to call the elevator when she heard steps around the corner and raced to the stairs to avoid being seen.

That night, she replayed the hit a hundred times in her dreams and was surprised the sight of the man's head exploding hadn't shocked her somehow. Seen too much violence on TV, she reckoned.

The man's death earned her a signed copy of Patricia Highsmith's early lesbian novel *The Price of Water*, which she had published under the name of Claire Morgan. Cornelia found the book profoundly disappointing once she got round to reading it a few days later.

No matter.

Nothing's perfect.

The next assignment that came up proved messier. She had to travel to Chicago and felt uncomfortable functioning in a different environment to her New York patch. It was a week-end job with Columbus Day added on. A woman on a dirty week-end with a Wall Street banker lover at the Drake Hotel. Establishing some sort of contact with her was a tough one. She couldn't use her seductive wiles and allure this time. She trailed the woman a whole day and managed to get a room next to the adulterous couple and, as she had been taught back at school, listened to their muted sounds of coupling by cupping her ear against the bottom of a glass which she held against the thin wall separating the hotel rooms. She felt a right fool. In the morning, after observing the clandestine couple sharing breakfast, Cornelia got her opportunity as the man and the woman separated and her target went on a shopping spree. It was touch and go but Cornelia didn't think she would get another chance. The woman was changing in a small cabin on the mezzanine floor of a Victoria's Secret branch on North Michigan. Cornelia knew it was too crowded to use the gun she had been provided with. Clad only in her underwear to avoid suspicion, she stepped from her own alcove toward the exiguous cabin where the other woman was changing. Fortunately, the other woman was short and slight so Cornelia had a height advantage. The whole operation was wordless. Before the target could protest at her intrusion, Cornelia had swished the scalpel straight across the woman's throat. The blood squirted everywhere. Over the floor, over Cornelia's white skin and garments, over the pile of discarded lingerie the woman had accumulated during the course of her shopping. But it had been the right method and no sound disturbed the changing area as Cornelia lowered the still spasming body to the floor. She quickly rushed back to her own alcove and slipped her suit on over the blood that still ran down her long limbs and slowly made her way to the street, trying not to attract attention.

Back at the hotel, she had to burn all the stained clothing, after cleaning herself in the shower. Then she took a cab to the airport after settling her bill. Cash, of course.

The mysterious intimate apparel murder even made the next day's newspapers. There was no suspect. The women in the store only had eyes for the lingerie, not for the other customers, particularly if other women's shapes proved slimmer or younger. Cornelia felt no need to keep the cuttings, though.

She suspected it was the cuckolded husband who had ordered the hit, but reckoned it wasn't for her to reason why. It was just a job, a means to an end. And the fee for the kill acquired her a set of early Modern Library firsts.

It was after the Chicago job that she asked the Organisation to change her status. From now onwards, she would only take a job on her own terms and time. She was surprised they accepted. She already had enough money in the bank for another six months with normal expenditure. She even cut the number of sets at the two clubs where she worked and steered clear of evening slots, where the customers were rowdier and keener to date her or have her more than just dance. The owners protested, but Cornelia gave them no choice. She knew by now she could easily find a job stripping in any joint in Manhattan. Told them she was resuming her studies, needed more time. They reluctantly agreed. After all, the wonderful Cornelia already had so many regulars who only came to watch her dance, and attracted a better class of customer, they reasoned.

She settled into a satisfactory routine. A few hours dancing a week, which paid for the rent, utilities and groceries, and the added income from her extra-curricular activities accounting for the luxuries: books and clothes.

Then there was Holly. Holly Fox.

Met in a bar, and her first real sex with another woman since early fumblings and stolen kisses in a school dormitory in her teens.

The night with Holly at the Gramercy Park apartment was one Cornelia would remember for a very long time. She had somehow never thought it would be so tender and enjoyable, and frenzied in its quiet acceptance of another kind of love. Cornelia danced for her. Holly had never been to a striptease show and had been completely taken by surprise when Cornelia had revealed her profession. So, all part and parcel of the rites of seduction, Cornelia had obliged with a particularly sensual private show.

In all honesty, Cornelia had never thought of herself as a lesbian, but now realised she was indeed bisexual, and was amazed that not everyone was. Being with a woman was good, different, although if pressed she would admit to the fact she would never be able to totally give up cock, even if the owners of the cocks seldom tickled her heart well enough to even contemplate a more permanent relationship than a one or two night stand. She liked to be filled. By something warm. And she enjoyed sucking cock. Relished the spongy texture, the heartbeat her tongue could always perceive under a cock's thin skin.

But Holly was nice and, for the first time in ages, Cornelia felt a need to spend more time with a person. She knew that

Holly could be both lover and friend; she could laugh with her, and fuck. The combination just felt so natural.

Which didn't stop her from mixing the powder with a night drink; and in the morning Holly was dead beside her.

At least she knew the woman's death had occurred painlessly, as she lay in her bed in the wake of a satisfying come, with hope and pleasure in her heart.

As a result, the first edition mint condition dust jacket of Malcolm Lowry's *Under the Volcano* became a bit of a sentimental favourite of Cornelia's, amongst all the books in her growing library.

From then on, Cornelia decided not to mix business with pleasure. It could only complicate things, make them messier. If she had to use her body to get close to a target, so be it, but only in the last resort. The killings had by necessity to remain impersonal, anonymous.

There was a guy in Brooklyn Heights. He fell through a window. Like a brick. Ernest Hemingway.

An Italian guy in Alphabet City. She'd been warned of his drug-taking. Doctoring the junk was child's play. Larry Clark's book of photographs of kids in Tulsa. Chillingly appropriate, she thought, but a mere coincidence. First she found the book, then she got the assignment.

But she preferred using guns. It was cleaner, more clinical, although she always had pangs of disappointment after every job when she had to dispose of the weapon she had used. But those were the rules. And they made sense.

She met a man. Maybe all the killings had melted her heart, rendered her vulnerable, but she tried to make it last longer. Going against ingrained habits. Gregory, his name was. Greg. It was nice while it lasted and she even thought of disconnecting from the Organisation. Dreams of tender domesticity and picket fences briefly clouded her thinking. But she had lied to him. A lot. When he discovered she stripped, he left.

Never again would she become close to anyone, she decided, and returned to her treadmill.

She hated the next job, in California. Disposing of an obnoxious porn filmmaker. In order to get close to him, she had to masquerade as an actress and got herself fucked every other way before she could retreat to the privacy of the house and retrieve her gun. Parading nude on the set, she had had no way to conceal it and was forced to go through with the whole disgusting charade. There were two studs present and she took great pleasure in executing them too. No way could they live and later boast how they had DP'ed this gorgeous New York stripper. She finished all three off with crotch shots before destroying the film which stored every minute of her infamy. F. Scott Fitzgerald's *Tender is the Night*. A very expensive acquisition, costing her more than she had wanted to pay.

The episode left a very bitter taste in her mouth for months and it wasn't until nearly half a year later that Cornelia allowed herself to be tempted by another book.

The job proved easy. Brooklyn. Faking a suicide. If the target had been cumbersome, she feared beforehand she might actually have to give up the whole contract killing caper. But by the time the Fredric Brown set proudly sat on her shelves in the Greenwich Village apartment she still lived in, she had put the past behind her and reconciled herself with the way things went.

The next kill was on her home patch of the Village, a British guy who seemed to know what was coming and offered no resistance. Because she had been given lines for him, she knew the job had been ordered by another woman. Whose name had to be the last word he heard. He took the bullet with a look of relief. It was following this easy assignment that Cornelia got herself the tattoo, in memory of the Sig Sauer she had used.

It appealed to her irony.
A small present to herself.
For keeps. Forever.
And, damn, it felt sexy.

3: Martin

The deep of night accepts no lies. In dreams, the truth. A persistent migraine, unrelieved by dissolving a couple of aspirins in a glass of fizzing Pepsi Cola, had forced an early night on me. As I fell asleep, I was already wrestling with daydreams and a kaleidoscope of images out of control rushing through the crowded turnpike of my mind, as I tossed and turned like an epileptic under the duvet, begging for closure, for the past to magically fade away if only temporarily.

The persistent, monotonous drip-drip of the rain outside the window punctuated my swirling thoughts of random events, women, places and sordid past cases.

Finally, all the ambient noises merged into utter silence: the rain falling on my leafy, suburban street, a floorboard in the corridor that sometimes creaked, the hot water flowing through the old central heating pipes, all the secret sounds of a house in darkness, magnified somehow in my highly-trained imagination. All became quiet, absolutely still.

I was dressed again, eating under-spiced food in an Athens taverna, bouzouki muzak punctuating the air, half-reading a book while stealing glances at a lone woman eating at another table and trying to guess her nationality. Her eyes meeting mine. Complicity. Loneliness. Jump cut to me fucking her in a hotel room (mine? hers?) and my gaze captured by a small, square plastic clothes label incongruously stuck to the very centre of her right butt as I sweatily thrust in and out of her cunt, oblivious to the obscenities she is spouting about how this lover of hers in Istanbul the week before lent her to a friend and watched them doing it. Hard inside her, my rhythm metronomic, insistently ploughing her stretched mid-western pussy, trying anxiously to decipher the writing on the label without losing my sexual concentration. She must have known she was on the pull tonight, I guessed: had slipped on brand new panties, not that I had given the flimsy garment any damn notice when undressing her in lustful frenzy. Cut. I was a child again, boiling inside at the sheer injustice of the world, lodged uncomfortably under my teacher's desk at primary school as punishment for something or other, red in the face at the thought of what the other school kids must be thinking, saying about me. Running around the playground time and again, my knees bruised, my chest on fire, imagining that I'm the Czech champion Emil Zatopek. Years later, swimming in a broad, dirty river, my heart full of the folk music of Joan Baez and Bob Dylan I've just discovered and thinking obsessively of Christel, the German exchange language student with whom I am platonically sharing a tent in nearby Fontainebleau forest this night. Christel who is four years older than me, already a woman, insisted I turn my back when I visited her in her garret flat amongst the Paris rooftops near the Gare d'Austerlitz, and she washed herself in the basin in the middle of the room. But I peeped. Of course. Christel whom I followed some months later to the Vallée de Chevreuse, seeking her at the youth hostel, but she didn't appear and, my heart asunder, I walked miles and miles seeking her on every farm or isolated café where she might be working before forlornly hitching back to Paris as night drew near. Flash forward to who knows when in the sad parade that was my life. A New York hotel room where I am thrusting in and out of the wrong woman and taking out my anger on her, my hands closing on her wrists and leaving dark marks, my teeth biting into her neck as I thrust violently in and out of her, it's not her fault, it's just that she's not the woman I want to be here, the one I crave for is back in London or is it Frankfurt, being ploughed doggie-style by her husband or some other fucking stranger. So I continue to batter the insides of the one I am with, from Finland she is but no longer lives there, I can feel my cock fully extended scraping against her innermost recesses, and she moans and she moans and I feel like screaming and telling her not you, not you. Out of the corner of my eye, I watch a small cockroach slide down the hotel room wall and move into my suitcase. I smile but I keep on fucking the woman. In New Orleans too, many years later, I saw a cockroach dance a slow tango on a wall. It was also a hotel room, there was also a woman with me in that room. I don't recall the sex we had, all I remember was that the air-conditioning was wonky and we had to change rooms twice. Slow fade. Teenagers in a circle on the carpeted floor of a Kensington mansion, playing a game of truth, and one guy whispers boastfully that he has had Catherine, small, adorable buck-toothed Catherine, and my heart sinks and I want to die as my whole sixteen-year old world collapses around me like planets colliding in the silent void of space. Flashback. My mother in a hospital bed, her face and body now but the shroud of a skeleton, eaten away inside by the cancer from the damn cigarettes, and me, not finding the right words to say, unable to conjure tears (they always come later) or any sign of emotion. The blankness of me. The inability to express pain on the outside. The coldness of me. The killer inside. Oh oh oh the memories are now on the rampage, like flaming battalions of marching ants ravaging my brain and there is so little I can do to stop their inexorable advance. I am asleep and I am awake and I am aware that I am the prisoner of a dream, of a film that unfolds and I can't reach the stop button on the damn VCR. And an insidious voice that comes from nowhere and everywhere keeps on flashing forward to the next section in the story, the one part I have no wish to experience again. Ever again. Eyes, a body, a voice, a woman who just melts my heart with the sheer shadow of a smile, a mole on her left breast or is it a birthmark, a tooth out of alignment, a small scar on her right cheek. No, I try to shout out loud, you are not welcome in this dream. You do not belong there. I probably twist my body convulsively around the bed and will her to not advance further into the dream. This is my dream. Mine only. So fuck off. Stay out of it. Stop torturing me. And somehow it works. For a moment at least. I will her away and the dream becomes the night and my heart stops and I die and it's a field of green that stretches beyond the horizon and I'm standing in the forest, looking out into the clearing. Everyone is dressed in black which makes no damn sense as it is pitch black, night, deep and devouring and black on black is just another contradiction, and what the hell I'm dead but I'm still here and I'm standing, my heart shattered into a thousand small pieces, like elements in an impossible jigsaw. I start walking. The ground beneath my black-socked feet is soft but dry. I am out of the forest. The others have now gone. I feel lost. I am lost. I turn my head around in all directions, looking for familiar bearings. There are none. The darkness is ever present. I close my eyes to listen to the night. I am blind, I am asleep, I am dead, I am deaf. Then a morsel of light appears, indistinct, distant, flickering on the screen rising under my eye-lids. I stop walking. I float among the darkness. So this is it, I catch myself thinking. The famous white light. The white pinhole slowly begins to expand. It is circular. Deep as a tunnel where the exit is still miles away. I relax. I have accepted the inevitable and am about to renounce all control over my body and senses when a voice, soft, vulnerable, just says 'hello', like on picking up the telephone. The voice. Her voice. It's above me, around me, behind me, ahead of me, inside me. Sounds like a long drawn out 'hello'. Hellooooo. Teasing almost, overflowing with quiet emotion, and I find myself torn between two directions, the white light that beckons and a woman who reminds me of things unfinished, of a closure that never really happened. The light grows stronger and I yearn for its blessed release, but all the time the words she says are being carved into my flesh with all the pain a kitchen knife cutting across skin can inflict and she is saying over and over and over again that this is just too easy, ain't it, that I can't get away like this, dying is too good for me. Dying is no solution. In the deepest recesses of sleep, I try to fight back the siren tones of her words because I know now that if I don't do something about it, fast, real fast, soon it will be more than her voice, it will be her face there in the darkness, her eyes, her pale naked body, and once again, unending loop of pain, I will have no choice, I will run towards her to beg for forgiveness, abandoning forever the embrace of the white light that would help me forget, that would cauterise my memory. I try to say something but my throat is sealed. I struggle to form words but my tongue is no longer there to help. I have to say something to her or I am lost. But already the light ahead of me is fading and the contours of her face are beginning to take shape. In all her heart-wrenching beauty. My silent scream is loud enough to wake the dead. Her face fades. And again I am asleep and again I am alive and again I am a world of insufferable pain.

I awoke from the nightmare, and all around me it still felt like hell. The mess of the bedroom, the smell and dampness of my own body baking between the dirty sheets and the winter duvet, the flashing red light of the radio alarm I hadn't reset since the day the electricity had been cut off at the mains while the engineer had installed the new digital box that now allowed the whole building to view a fantabulous forty-nine channels. Flying across the wide screen of my mind were all

the memories that just wouldn't go away and kept on relent-
lessly crisscrossing my neurones like imps dancing at
Halloween with large wooden brooms stuck up their arses. I
checked my watch, my status symbol and obscenely expensive Tag Heuer. It was late enough. Time to get up and go to
work.

It was the sort of leafy, quiet street where the cheapest house
would have cost the average punter a lifetime of salary
cheques as well as the total proceeds minus pimp commission
for selling both his mother and younger sister into slavery. A
metal gate protected the courtyard from the rest of the riff-
raff that roamed this neighbourhood between Swiss Cottage
and Regent's Park. I announced myself through the intercom
and the gate opened and I made my way through of flock of
polished BMWs and Volvos to the front door of the house.
Nola Poshard was waiting for me here.
    'Good morning to you, Mr Jackson.'
    'Ms Poshard.'
    'Did you sleep well?' she asked me.
    No point in lying.
    'Actually, no,' I answered.
    She didn't bother to ask me why.
    Not that I would have told her.
    A man has to have his privacy.
    'So...' she broke the awkward silence and led me to a large
room that looked back on a surprisingly large garden consid-
ering the part of town we were in. 'What is it you need now,
to begin your investigation in earnest?'
    I looked around the room. Modern furniture. Chrome and
dark wood and unsettling geometry. Philippe Starck maybe.
Tasteful prints in glass frames scattered across the walls.
Watercolours, sketches. From where I was couldn't quite dis-
tinguish the subject of most of them. Maybe I did need new

glasses. But nowhere could I see books. For someone who was intent on retrieving a rare book, Nola Poshard didn't appear particularly sold on displaying the manifold joys of literature.

I took my place on one of the leather couches.

She was wearing black leggings – no, too thin; stockings or tights I decided – and an outsize green sweatshirt that ended midway down her thighs. She knew she had great legs. You don't, or at any rate shouldn't, wear leggings otherwise.

'I haven't much to go on, you know,' I finally told her.

'I realise that. What can I do to help? I really want her found.'

'And the Le Carré book?'

'Of course.'

She took a cigarette from a pack open on a close-by antique desk. Damn, I hated women who smoked. Spoilt the kissing. Not that I even thought I had the slightest chance to ever lock lips with Nola Poshard, femme fatale and ice queen of this parish.

'Tell me everything about her, warts and all' I suggested. 'I need to get some mental picture.'

'You've seen her photos I left with you, haven't you? And I told you everything yesterday anyway.'

'Yes,' I said. 'But it's not enough. It's not just what Louise looks like. Tell me a bit about what makes her tick, her past, her habits, good and bad, the sort of men she likes, the perfumes she wears, the way she dresses, her taste in booze or drugs, her favourite clothes... All the things that make her Louise.'

'Gee, Mr Jackson, I don't know where to begin.'

'Call me Martin,' I said.

'I'd rather not,' she answered. 'Let's keep this on a purely professional level, can we?'

'OK,' I nodded. 'So tell me about Louise.'

How do you condense a person's life into words? Nola gave me the chronology, the details of family betrayals and outside episodes of lust, guilt and happenstance that had caused Louise's arrival and a deep-seated sense of envy between the two sisters. But it felt like another world, a sordid veneer of facts, things that had happened to others, and I felt no connection. The story, as she monotonously intoned it as she sat close to me, was just a confection of words. On their own, they made a sort of bizarre sense. Together, I couldn't grasp them and their implications. Was I in the wrong job? The hem of Nola's shirt kept on moving up as she spoke, the occasional flurry of her hands as she sought to emphasise a point of history pulling the thin material a little further up her thighs. My gaze rested on her knees, and the pale outline of a scar on the left knee – a childhood fall? – captured my attention. She spoke of Louise's perversity, how she flirted with older men from an early age, tested her sexual powers on them with wicked insolence, but it was the sort of tale I had heard a thousand times before. I knew there was no point in trying to understand the sexuality of younger women, it just made no sense and had to be accepted wholesale with all the other wonders and contradictions of the world. Some men had the key, I'd never had. But beyond the bare bones of Nola's diatribe against her younger half-sister, I could now sense what was missing here: emotions. A sense of a real person, with flesh, bones and feelings.

I interrupted the monologue.

'OK,' I said.

'OK what?' Nola queried.

'OK,' I repeated. 'I think that's all I require for now.' A thought occurred to me. 'Could I see her room?'

'Her room? There's nothing there. Don't think I haven't searched it thoroughly.'

'I'm sure you have,' I told her. 'But I would still like to see it, you know, spend some time there. Detecting is a bit of an impressionist patch,' I explained to Nola, 'not just information: little touches, intuition, details both important and casual. You just never know what is going to provide a lead, a direction. People always betray themselves in the small details. What they least expect often betrays them.'

'I see,' she acknowledged.

'Please,' I insisted. 'And I'd like to spend time alone there.'

'Fine,' she finally agreed. 'If that's you want. You're the investigator.'

'And you're the client, Ms Poshard.'

A young girl's room. Who has since become a woman. In this room? In this bed? With a man, a boy her own age or an older one? Pastel shades, soft furniture. A bedspread with flower motifs, matching pillows. Dolls and old teddies still piled up in one corner. Fading stationery on a wicker desk, with Hello Teddy motifs. Inside the drawer: hardening sticks of spearmint gum, yellowing photos of school friends, parents, even Nola still vampish ten years or so earlier in a garden by a pool about to jump, a broad grin addressed to the camera. Polaroids of a dog. Pencils in need of sharpening. Dust. Eraser debris. I closed the wicker drawer; never thought I'd find a diary still there. 'Dear Diary, I'm about to steal the book to spite that damn sister of mine and god knows what else and I am running away. I'll be staying at 218bis rue Saint Denis in Paris where I expect the detective she hires to find me, but only after I've fucked every man there under forty.' I smelled the room, hunting the distant fragrance of Louise's childhood, her loves, pains and fears. With the dust came a mixture of scents, dead flowers, green notes, a sharp acidy tang, soap fading against soft skin, anger, sadness. Briefly I thought I recognised one of the strands: Anaïs Anaïs maybe, but then it was gone. I moved to the bed. The sheets were immaculate, the bed had been changed since Louise's hasty departure and clean linen substituted. Never mind, I was no expert in reading cum or secretion stains or sufficiently Sherlock Holmes-like in coming up with mighty deductions from the differing pubic hairs still scattered across a tired set of sheets. I slipped a hand between the mattress and the bed's frame. Nothing. Too obvious.

An old Compaq sat on the dressing table. I switched it on, lingered pensively while it booted up and explored the computer's memory. There was nothing there, all files had been erased as far as I could see. I unscrewed the back of the machine and pulled the hard drive out. I knew a company in Wandsworth who could do wonders extricating information from seemingly censored corners.

The scent of her soap was, naturally, stronger in the small en-suite bathroom, even though the cleaners (or Louise, prior to her departure) had thoroughly cleared it of cosmetics, left-over soap bars and even towels. I nosed around, my mind clutching at straws. The cabinet still held some unsuspicious run-of-the-mill medicine: soluble Disprin tablets, shocking pink Ibuprofen pills, Migraleve tablets, a toothpaste dispenser, tubes of lip salve, spare toothbrushes. The fixtures were standard, the shower curtain plastic and opaque. I had an idea and stepped over to the toilet and lifted the top of the porcelain cistern. Bingo. Lodged behind the plastic float was a wodge of plastic. I pulled it out. Ah, the influence of bad movies!

It wasn't a gun, or the hoped-for diary full of gushing revelations, but a bundle of postcards. All from foreign cities, addressed to Louise care of a PO box at what appeared to be a nearby post office, and each in the same distinctive, cursive handwriting.

I disposed of the plastic wrapping in the bin and slipped the handful of cards into my jacket pocket.

The text revealed little.

Endearments. Fantasies. Feelings. 'I miss you'. 'I want you'. 'Wish you were here'. 'If only'. 'A city without you.'

A man of few words.

Amsterdam. New York. New Orleans. Seattle. An interesting mix. The family, I recalled, had its roots in Louisiana.

I turned my back on Louise's room and made my way down the stairs. Nola still sat where I had left her, deep in thought, draped over the heavy leather sofa. The level of her hem was now approaching indecency, not that discovering whether she was wearing tights or stockings would make any difference to my libido.

'I'm done,' I told her.

'See yourself out, then, Mr Jackson.'

She barely looked up at me.

'I will report back as soon as I have any worthwhile information, Ms Poshard.'

'I do hope so,' she said.

'Trust me, I'm a detective,' I said as I walked towards the front door and Regent's Park.

The femme fatale of the parish didn't even smile.

Cold-hearted, I decided.

And there was the problem in a nutshell. Cold-hearted women turned me on, and right now, in the taxi threading its way through the midday rush hour along Wigmore Street, I had an appetite for sex.

This is where the mean street crusader in most stories picks up the phone, and after a a quick browse through his little black book suggests a chat over drinks about past times to some old flame, or some pliant assistant who's absolutely besotted with him. I had neither mobile phone nor secretary and the last woman who'd taken me to her bed was highly unlikely to repeat the invitation. In fact, I was desperately trying not to think of her. She'd fucking broken my heart and more.

I tapped on the partition and alerted the cab driver.

'Change of direction, mate. Can you take me to Waterloo?'

He turned into Baker Street and the traffic we encountered became even thicker.

Darkness comes earlier at this time of year and even though it was barely three in the afternoon, the lateness of the season and the heavy grey skies combined in a false dusk as we reached the railway station's zone of concrete bunkers.

I had the driver drop me off in the shadow of the Millennium Wheel and made the rest of the journey to the railway arches by foot. The entrance to the Kubla Khan was in a slight recess, and the sign advertising the presence of the health club was discreet in the extreme and most passers-by would not even notice it.

I paid my ten pounds entrance fee and signed myself in. Mike Smith. This was an establishment which was big with the worldwide family of Smith. The attendant didn't even look up at my face. Well-trained in the art of discretion.

I was handed two medium size white towels and a locker key attached to a thick rubber band, and shown the way to the changing room.

Sitting on the wooden bench surrounded by a gallery of upright lockers, I undressed. A black guy was doing likewise in another corner of the small room. He nodded silently at me as he pulled his boxers off to reveal a somewhat awesome penis which appeared to be already semi erect. Or at least I hoped it was. He smiled as my gaze locked on his cock. 'You like?' he asked.

'Nice,' I said. I had no wish to offend him. The rest of his body was particularly fit; toned muscles rippling along his back as he bent over to slip the rubber band holding his locker key around his ankle. So that's what the rubber band was for.

I slipped my T-shirt off, then my socks. I was sorely conscious of the fact that inside my final piece of underwear I was still quite small and limp.

'First time here, eh?' the black guy called out.

'Yeah.'

'Nice place. You'll like it. Very relaxed,' he said.

I pulled my briefs down past my ankles. Threw the garment and rest of my clothes inside the locker and stood, naked, to turn the key in the lock.

He was watching me do this while tieing one of his own towels around his midriff. I did likewise. I began stretching the key's thick rubber band across my foot and towards my ankle.

'You top or bottom?' the black guy said.

'Switch,' I answered, and then added, 'but sometimes prefer to be bottom.'

'In that case, you'd better put the band around your wrist, man,' he said. 'It's a code. If you're looking for action, if you know what I mean.'

I straightened up and inserted my left hand through the rubber band's girth.

The black guy laughed and left the changing room. I adjusted the towel around me. I had to push my stomach out to keep it fixed around my waist. I walked out into the corridor leading to the facilities.

The shower area was in semi darkness and empty right now, which gave me courage as I dropped my towel to a bench and thoroughly cleaned myself after getting the balance between hot and cold water right following some halting experimentation. Other men came and went as I washed. Few of them even bothered to cover themselves with towels. They came in all shapes and sizes. Quite a few orientals, some younger men with skinhead cuts and tattoos. Finally, I left the shower, dried myself and ventured further into the innards of the health club. The first sauna room was rather crowded but I found myself a place on the edge of one of the wooden benches. The man next to me was openly playing with himself. It was so dark in there that, beyond him, I could barely see the white outline of the other bodies present. But soon the heat got to me and I was gasping for breath. It had been years since I'd been to a sauna, and I had forgotten how the air was so thin and the heat attacked you all the way down your throat. I closed my eyes, hoping to surmount the feeling of oppression, but failed abysmally. The burn inside was moving down towards my lungs. I rose to my feet and made my way to the door. As I did, a hand in the darkness brushed against my cock and muttered something unintelligible.

Outside again, I caught my breath, relaxed. Then realised I'd left my towel in the overheated cabin. The other one I'd been given was in the locker. I reckoned I didn't need it yet and delved further into the darkness of the Kubla Khan. A second sauna cabin on my left appeared even more crowded and smaller than the first. Through the glass window all one could see was a jumble of bodies, and much movement. I passed. Down the corridor I could see a brighter-lit window. The steam room. Approaching, I noted a phalanx of bodies dotted around the periphery of the humid, misty room.

What the hell, I thought, let's see how low I can go. It didn't matter anyway. Kay was gone from my life forever and I knew I had to take the punishment in some form or other.

Naked, I entered the steam room.

Within a minute or two of seating myself at the edge of one of the benches, the man next to me began caressing my cock. I said nothing. Allowed him to continue. Soon, I was hard as he handled me with due care and attention, caressing my shaft within his clenched fingers, delicately slipping a finger across my glans. Amidst the whiteness of the steam room, I turned my head to see who he was. Just another man, middle-aged, a trifle overweight, with early signs of baldness. As he wanked me with his left hand, his right one played with his own cock which jutted out from the fold of his lower stomach and the curly bush of his pubic hair, thick, uncut, the mushroom head a darker hue of purple than mine. He was looking straight ahead of him, into the cloud of steam that floated there, as if I didn't even exist and his hand was manipulating a toy, an object. I felt no excitement as he handled me, his busy hands ignorant of the rhythm my pleasure required. This went on for another minute in absolute silence. Then, there was a grunt and through a clearing in the steam I saw another white body kneeling on the stone floor just a couple of metres away from me, and as my vision improved I realised the man was sucking another off, his head bobbing up and down in the lap of, I thought, the black guy who had greeted me in the changing room. The sound had come from the throat of the coloured man being pleasured. Had he just come in the other's mouth? The steam surrounded them again.

I moved my right hand in the direction of the lap of the man jerking me off and, hearing no objection, took hold of his penis, brushing his own hand away. Felt rubbery, not quite what I'd expected. Clumsily, I fingered his humid foreskin, then his shaft, trying to remember the way I liked women to touch me there.

'Suck me,' he soon whispered in my ear, leaning towards me, his hand deserting my cock and lingering across the small of my back as my manual attempts at playing with him floundered.

I didn't even hesitate. I knew from the moment I had

entered the health club that I would go with the flow, to the
bitter end of this. My hand moved away from his cock and I
rose from the wooden bench, placed myself on my knees on
the slippery surface of the floor and drew my face level with
his crotch. The middle-aged stranger adjusted his position by
opening his legs wider. I moved my head forward.

He held his cock aloft.

I opened my mouth and took him whole.

I sucked him with eyes closed. I could feel the texture of
his skin, the difference between glans, stretched foreskin and
the rougher surface of the shaft as my tongue explored him
slowly. From time to time, he would thrust his crotch
forward, the cock digging deep into the back of my throat
and I had to react quickly and modify my angle of suction to
avoid choking. Actually, I reflected, it wasn't that unpleasant.
But neither was it pleasurable. This I knew both instinctively
and because my own cock had detumesced and shrunk. I
applied myself to the fellation, wondering when he would
come and whether I would have to swallow it. He stayed
hard, and warm, inside my mouth and as my tongue slithered
up and down the shaft, I thought I could feel the beating of his
heart as I moved along the darker veins that crisscrossed his
cock.

Right then, there was movement behind me and I felt a
touch on the nape of my neck, a kiss. From another stranger.
Then a hand cupped my buttocks, and a finger was drawn
down the crack of my arse. My mouth intimately attached to
the cock of the sitting man, I was unable to react to this new
contact and didn't break the heavy silence of the steam room.
A wet finger dug itself, nail and all, past my anal sphincter
and broke into me. I tried to relax my muscles, to allow it
passage.

I had just adjusted to this penetration when the man I was
sucking pushed my head away and rose and, without a

further word, still erect, walked out of the steam room. The man who was skewering my rear behind me bade me to rise and his body rubbed itself against me. His finger abandoned my anus and I could feel the hardness of his member press against my buttocks. For a few moments, we both stood there while he rubbed against me, his body felt all greased up. I tried to turn my head to see who he was, but with a hand, he indicated I should stay still. Finally, I heard him say 'I have a condom; come upstairs with me.'

I did.

There was a row of cabins of different sizes under a low, dark ceiling. Each had a plastic mattress. He held me by my cock, like a dog on a leash as we walked up the narrow metal stairs to the private cabins. He selected one of the more spacious ones and led me inside.

'Do you want privacy?' he asked.

'I'm not bothered,' I answered quietly.

He left the swing door to the cabin open. As he pushed me to my knees onto the cold mattress, I saw the shadows of other men grouping themselves by the door to our cabin, to watch.

My partner, a skinny guy with a smooth chest and a long thin cock, presented his penis to my mouth and I accepted it. It was easy after the first time. I sucked him with a semblance of vigour until he was rock hard. I could hear his breath grow more shallow as I did so. Out of the corner of my eye, I noticed he had a blurred tattoo on his left arm and saw that some of the men outside the cabin watching me sucking him were playing with themselves.

'Now,' he said.

He positioned me on the mattress, applied some cream to my opening and placed his cock at its point of entry. One thrust and he was inside me. I was surprised it didn't even hurt. And then the stranger fucked me. I didn't even know whether he was wearing a condom or not. Once again, I felt no pleasure, wondered what all the fuss was about, what kicks other men got out of being buggered, forced, but I also knew I was being too analytical about this. He moved rapidly inside me. Just felt like taking a shit in reverse really. Being stuffed, dilated further with every one of his thrusts. One of the men by the open swing door approached and presented his cock to my mouth, as I was being shaken by the forward movements of the man fucking me. I shook my head to decline but he wouldn't take no for an answer and his penis soon breached my lips. One more, or less I figured. Now I was being truly fucked. But a few perfunctory licks of my tongue against his pee hole and he withdrew with a jerk and I felt his come splash against my chin and upper chest. And I felt a warm sensation inside my arse as the first stranger also came.

A minute or so later, I was already on my own on the mattress, my two transitory partners gone, the spectators departed for other spectacles and the ejaculate dripping out of me and down my legs.

In a way, it had been too easy.

Like so many other things, was this all there was to it? I wondered as I washed away all the traces of my usage in the shower downstairs.

By the time I hit the street outside, a sea of commuters was marching from all directions into the maw of Waterloo Station as dusk settled over the London grey.

4: Martin

The computer screen flickered blue as I settled my backside into the leather comfort of my designer armchair.
Joan had called in. Chicken pox. She'd be away for a few weeks. Hoped I'd cope on my own.

I'd manage. Batman without his Robin.

Who needs a sidekick anyway?

I connected with the various search engines and systematically explored all the key areas of the case: the Poshard family, book collecting and recent auctions, the cities that appeared to be at the epicentre of the affair.

Hundreds of bytes of information flowed across the screen and I began the necessary process of elimination.

Martin Jackson, Internet Detective! Made me sound like the valiant hero of a pre-war pulp magazine. See him surf, see him crash, see him find the woman (and preferably the missing book)!

The phone rang. It was Christopher Streetfield, wanting to know what progress I had made in locating his missing wife. I pacified him.

'Not much to go on, Mr Streetfield,' I said. 'But there are one or two avenues I'm looking into. Some possibilities. I will get back to you as soon as I have something positive. I just don't believe in making uneccessary promises or raising my clients' hopes in vain.'

'I fully understand,' he agreed.

He was off to Norway the next day for his work, and provided me with his coordinates there.

'I'll keep my mobile charged up, so you can contact me

any time while there,' he added, with a touch of gentle desperation.

'OK.'

I put the phone down. I felt no guilt about lying to him so blatantly. Since the moment I had accepted the assignment I had had no intention whatsoever of investigating his wife's disappearance. How could he not read it all over my face? Are all cuckolds so blind?

I returned to the web.

It was like reading tea leaves. So much junk, so much detail, but you had to narrow in, focus on some small clues here and there and try and make sense of it all. The previous year, a crooked telecom executive had sold me various codes and I was now able to hack in to a number of databases with full access to a welter of financial and personal records. It had been a perfect investment, and half of my successful cases since had unravelled across my screen, the pieces of who had done what to who or stolen this from that or checked into the wrong hotel with the wrong partner had unfolded ever so easily amongst the lingering tracks of credit card transactions. What a detective needed these days was a keyboard, not a gun.

First, there was a piece of information here that appeared of interest, then another there, then yet more items amongst the undigested, unedited load of information floating out in cyberspace, hidden like nuggets of gold between the flotsam and the useless shit that crowded the information highway. One thing led to to another and then again further down the pixel road; as my fingers danced an elaborate waltz over the keyboard, I avoided the dead-ends, the branches in the road that looked as if they would lead nowhere, and began making some vague sense of the whole farrago, translating intuitions into hard fact. It was at least three hours until I looked up from the screen again. Yes, certainly some interesting leads. Names that connected to the Poshard family that somehow shouldn't;

curious connections; unexplained oddities in various recent book auctions. I blinked, rubbed my eyes. Walked over to the small fridge I kept in the far corner of the office. In a *noir* novel, I would have kept my booze there, the traditional bottle of whisky or bourbon, or maybe a gun in the ice compartment. Instead, I broke off a chunk of Brie cheese and gulped it down, followed by a sip from the cola bottle I kept at the foot of my desk. I returned to the computer screen, connected it to the printer, loaded it up with paper, scrolled along the relevant lines and clicked. For the real work, the hours of peering at words and data, I still needed old-fashioned sheets of paper.

Soon, I'd downloaded all I needed from the day's trawl.

Time for the leg work to begin, I reckoned. Never my favourite part of sleuthing.

A few telephone calls for flight and hotel bookings and I was ready. I sat there, pensive, thinking ahead, still trying somehow to erase the past beating at the doors of my brain. I ignored an incoming call, as I was certain it was Christopher Streetfield, again chasing me about the damn case of the missing wife. Who did he think I was, Perry Mason?

He didn't leave a message, but I recognised his number as it scrolled along the thin LED line.

Damn him, why couldn't he try and forget about her?

I must have sat there for at least another couple of hours, thinking of nothing in particular, unable to void my mind completely. Pangs of hunger brought me back to reality.

I put the print-outs into a folder and placed this inside my Samsonite case. As an afterthought, maybe a case of professional integrity, I also gathered the Streetfield papers, still unread in their manila envelope, from the drawer I'd banished them to and dropped them in. After all, the fool had actually paid me some cash to do his impossible job.

Alongside the train, the motorway into Amsterdam was jampacked with cars, slowly sputtering along in the early evening gloom. A good thing I'd remembered that the train from Schipol was both faster and cheaper. Soon, I was making my way through the bowels of the Central Station, an anonymous middle-aged man dressed in black, quietly invisible between the backpackers, the housewives from the provinces and an assortment of luggage-laden tourists that preceded the rush hour commuter traffic out of the city. The cold beat a way through to my very bones as I crossed the first canal and the wind assaulted me at full-frontal strength.

I quickened my step and made for Leidseplein.

The first appointment I'd set up was for the following morning so I had the evening free. I set up the laptop in my hotel bedroom and checked my e-mails, then took a warm shower and changed into a warmer shirt. All I was planning was a meal, maybe an Indonesian – I hadn't been to Amsterdam for years – then an early night. Possibly pick up a hardcore mag or two, you could find them all over town, and wank myself to sleep.

It was the way the young woman in the hotel bar looked me straight in the eyes as I walked out of the lift that caught my attention.

She seemed lost, her soft blue eyes begging for attention with quiet despair. She wore a black trouser suit and a grey chenille sweater and her hair was short, brown with gentle blonde streaks. First impression was that she was just a teenager, but as I held her gaze I quickly realised she was much older. There was a dignity in her stance that touched me. If she was on the make, her face distinctly said that this wasn't the sort of thing she was accustomed to.

Instead of moving through the lobby and out onto the street, I stepped over to the hotel bar. I was in no rush to face the bitter cold outside.

Her eyes followed my path.

'Hello,' I said.

'Hello,' she answered. She had a strong accent. But it wasn't Dutch, I knew.

'I'm Martin. Are you alone?'

'Yes.'

'Can I join you? Offer you a drink?'

'Sure,' she said. 'My name is Aida.'

'Where do you come from?' I asked her, easing myself into the chair next to hers.

'Lithuania,' she answered.

'Interesting. But your name makes you sound Egyptian,' I pointed out.

'I know. My mother liked the opera.'

'Verdi?'

'Yes.'

She ordered a glass of red wine while I stuck to mineral water.

'From Vilnius?' I inquired.

'You know?'

'Know of it. Never been there,' I told her.

'Most people think I'm Russian. It's all the same for them,' Aida said.

She had lovely cheekbones.

'So what are you doing in Holland?' I asked. 'You're a long way from home.'

'A man. Met a Dutch man,' she informed me, but her tone of voice sounded bruised.

'Where is he now?'

She studiously sipped her wine. Even sitting there, she appeared tall. Slim, small-chested and a touch nervous, it seemed to me.

'At home.'

'You still live with him? Married?'

'Yes. No,' Aida said.

'Care to clarify that?' I smiled.

'He's my ex. But I still live in his house.'

'I see.'

'I have a little boy. Two years old.'

'With him?'

'Yes. But since I had the baby, I just don't love him any more. We don't have sex any more. We live by the sea. It's a very small house; we have to share the bedroom.'

She lowered her eyes.

'So what brings you to Amsterdam today?'

'I'm not sure I should tell you,' she said, looking up at me again. Her eyes seemed to float between grey and blue.

'You don't have to,' I tried to reassure her. 'After all, I'm just a man talking to a woman he doesn't know in a hotel bar, and by tomorrow no doubt we will be strangers again.' I don't know why I suddenly said that. My problem is I've always been too fatalistic or seen too many movies and should have learned long ago that life is nothing like films.

'Wow!' Aida said.

'Sorry, that was a silly thing for me to say.'

'No, I liked,' Aida replied, the trace of a smile taking shape across her full lips.

'Good.' I smiled back, as sincerely as I could manage.

'Well, three days a week I work in the chocolate factory. But most of the money I earn goes towards paying the baby sitter and I want to get a place of my own for myself and the baby,' Aida said. 'So I was thinking of earning more money...' Her words faded away and she looked down at her knees again.

'How?' I asked.

'I just cannot live with him any more. Since I told him I didn't want him, he frightens me. He's, what you call it, manic depressive and I'm afraid one day he might harm me and the baby.'

'Do you really think he would? His own child?'

'Last summer, I met a Swiss man on the Internet and went to live with him, in Bern, for a few weeks. He was very angry when I did that. But I tell him I cannot love him any more.'

'What happened to the Swiss guy?' I inquired.

She finished her wine and carefully set the glass down on the bar.

'It was a mistake. He just wasn't right for me…'

'How?'

'It's only when you live with someone you really find out about all their habits. At first, he was nice, it made a change, but soon he began to irritate me, small things, always a maniac about timekeeping, orderliness, those sort of things.'

I ordered Aida another glass of wine with a nod of the head towards the hotel barman.

'Sexually? Was it OK?' I asked.

'It was different, but not enough to make me stay,' she replied, holding my gaze.

'So you came back to your Dutch boyfriend?'

'Yes… I had nowhere else to go. '

'Lithuania? Family?'

'Marcel wouldn't let me take the baby away.'

'So, do you do this often?' I asked Aida.

'Do what?' she was visibly puzzled by my question.

'Meet men in hotel bars?'

She blushed deeply.

Blurted it out, and it was obviously the truth.

'It's the first time,' she said.

'Really?' I insisted.

'Yes. I walked round the red light district this afternoon, watching the women in their windows, wondering whether I could ever do that. I was thinking of talking to one, asking what I should do, but I got frightened. Just couldn't find the courage to appear in a window under a bright light exposing myself as they do and selling my body to any man who would want me. I just wouldn't be able to cope with older ones, the ugly ones... Silly, no?'

'Not at all. It would be a momentous decision to take,' I said.

'Have you ever been with a prostitute?' Aida asked.

'Yes,' I admitted. 'I was nineteen.'

'Nineteen would be good,' Aida said. 'I wouldn't mind too much.'

'It was too fast, too mechanical. There was no tenderness. Just a financial transaction,' I told her. 'How old are you, Aida?'

'I was twenty-eight two weeks ago,' she answered.

'I like you Aida,' I said. 'But I wouldn't pay you money. I decided I would never do that again, since that first time.'

'I guessed so.' She shifted her legs, her body still facing me alongside the bar.

'There must be other ways to earn money,' I ventured.

'Yes,' Aida said. 'But not enough. My Dutch is not good enough. Maybe as receptionist in a hotel...'

'Hmm, yes, your conversational English is quite good.'

'But unless there was somewhere to stay, an apartment that came with the job, and the little boy, Nidas, was old enough to go to school, it wouldn't be enough to stay independent.'

'You've thought about it a lot, I see.'

'Yes. Before you arrived, I was sitting here thinking of solutions. Maybe I should put an ad in a newspaper, offering myself as a mistress to an older man, who could give me a place. I could give him sex.'

'It's a bit drastic solution-wise,' I pointed out. 'I'm sure there must be better opportunities.'

She looked up at me and in the penumbra of the bar, the tip of her nose shone and her vulnerability assaulted me with all the strength of an emotional whirlpool. Instinctively, I took her hand and mine.

'Your hand is so warm,' she remarked.

'I know.'

There was a moment's silence while our thoughts swirled around the bar in a hesitation dance that only we two could see. For a minute or so I wrestled with my conscience, or what was left of it, as I pondered whether I should pay her after all. Something about her attracted me. A lot. It was only money, after all. I had it. She wanted it. I wanted sex. And she was no common street whore; just a clumsy, touching amateur. By tomorrow night I would already be out of Amsterdam. What the hell? My resolve was changing. But Aida beat me to it.

'I like you too,' she said. 'You are... different from other men, I think.'

We went to my room.

She had been wearing a padded bra and her breasts were slighter than I had guessed. I found them adorable. A dark beauty spot stared at me from the underside of her left nipple, a perfect touch of imperfection that tugged at my heart, as I licked and sucked on her teat like a new-born child and listened to her gentle moans. She lay on the bed, passive, naked to the waist down after we had kissed for an eternity, standing in the narrow corridor that led from the door to the actual bedroom, tongue assaulting tongue as if our lives depended on it. With every new assault of my lips on her open mouth, I could feel her shudder. Either out of nervousness or lust, but her reaction encouraged me to delve further down her throat, to grip her tongue in my suction or drill my own tongue even further down. She responded sweetly, a hand brushing across my unruly hair as I embraced her, our bodies pressing against each other, every heartbeat amplified through the material of our clothes, every degree of heat created by our desire bathing us in its glow. Lips still attached, I had allowed my fingers to roam under her chenille sweater and had, after a couple of clumsy attempts, managed to unclasp her bra and loosen its hold. Then I had detached myself from her and straightened her arms above her head and tugged the sweater off and gently pulled her along to the bed and helped her position herself over the silky cover and resumed our urgent mouth contact.

'OK?' I whispered, catching my breath between kisses, two of my fingers kneading a nipple into hardness.

'Yes,' Aida said. 'Very.'

'Good.'

'No man has ever kissed me like you do,' she continued, a gentle smile spreading across her features and her eyes bluer than ever.

A perfect invitation to continue.

My head lowered itself towards her face, and my free hand slid under the waistband of her black trousers, fingers soon stumbling against the bush of her crotch. Hot, humid, hungry. I breathed deeply as her reaction coursed from her genitals all through her body and her lips fluttered as they rubbed against mine.

I detached myself from Aida and knelt by the foot of the bed and unbuttoned her trousers. Pulling them off, she raised her rump to assist my undressing her. She was wearing pristine white knickers and when I rolled her around, I saw they were thongs and a lone small pink pimple adorned her left bum cheek. I couldn't resist licking it, kissing her flaws with all the affection I could muster. She undid my shirt and we resumed our feverish but unhurried embrace. She remained silent. So did I. Words were no longer required.

I had resisted the temptation too long as I partook of Aida's sweet full lips at lazy leisure, but I finally slipped the final white garment off her long, slim body and uncovered her cunt. Her thin curls had recently been trimmed into a tidy triangle (in preparation for tonight's much-thought-of accession to whoredom?). I buried my face in it, my nose digging deep into the hair and skin, eager for the scent of her intimacy. There was barely the trace of a smell, which initially surprised me. I withdrew my face and looked into her ultimate privacy. Her labia protruded slightly from the her pubic thatch, a dark pink gash in the core of her inner darkness. I put out a finger and parted her. Immediately I felt her abundant wetness and my digit sunk in deep into the heat of her small furnace. Inside, Aida was on fire. I moved my lips closer again and traced her gash with my tongue, tasting her unique mustiness. Quickly her labia filled and I plunged my tongue into her depths and began to suck on the loose folds of her flesh. Lower down the cunt opening, thick ridges of puckered, soft, darker skin surged outward like the roll of a small hill. I soon located her clitoris and sucked it out of its bud and chewed away. Tremors ran through her body from top to bottom and I spread her legs open around my head and invaded her with my fingers. She was a quiet one, neither a shouter or a moaner, but then again she couldn't disguise the pleasure I was providing her with, and each time I came up for air she let her breath out momentarily, as if asking me not to stop.

One time, she actually whispered 'Stop teasing me, please.'

Finally, she began shaking uncontrollably and came.

I kissed Aida. Her eyes shone. I had left the bedroom light on throughout.

I moved away from her and stood up and rid myself of the rest of my clothes and lowered myself beside her. Squashed myself against her on the exiguous single bed, enjoying all the joyful heat radiating from her naked flesh. She soon slithered away from me, reversed her position and unhesitatingly took my cock into her mouth and began hungrily lapping at it.

Unlike many women, she did not take the shaft in her hand to minimise its length, but gripped my buttocks and impaled her mouth on me, taking all of my penis deep inside her without choking. She worked fast on it, gobbling it up and down with wonderful, childlike relish, even though I was not totally hard yet. Too many thoughts crowded my mind, fighting a complete erection, of others, of Kay, of times before, of the way women whose faces or names I could not recall had fellated me before. But few had done so with such enjoyable abandon, I knew.

Finally, I knew it was time, and I extricated myself from her avid lips and positioned myself above her and prepared to enter her.

'Haven't you got a condom?' she asked.

'No, Aida,' I replied. 'I somehow hadn't prepared for this encounter, you know.'

'It's OK, I have one in my handbag,' she said.

She got up and walked over to the bag she had left on the coat hanger by the door and returned quickly. Her naked body in motion looked so enticing and I felt myself attaining full hardness. Small hanging breasts, solid rump, thin legs and a graceful movement of the hips as she moved from and back to the bed, her skin so pale and white and already dripping with sweat.

'You have a lovely cock,' Aida said, as she unrolled the condom. 'I've never had a man with a, what you call it, circul... circom...'

'Circumcised,' I helped her out, wondering what the word was in Lithuanian.

'Circumcised cock... It looks so... cute,' she said. She began rolling the thin latex across my glans. 'What does it feel like to be like that?' she asked.

'I'm not sure I can answer that question,' I told her. 'I've never had a chance to compare, you know.'

She giggled and completed her task.

'I like it doggy-style,' she said. 'Please.'

She turned round and I finally entered her with a single thrust.

The first fuck with Aida was good and we unbelievingly came together. The combined view of her white arse shuddering while my cock buried itself inside her was heavenly, pornographic. I watched with hypnotic concentration as the darker ring of her anus sometimes dilated slightly as my cock dug deeper into her and, just before I lost all control, actually slipped a finger inside her there where it fitted effortlessly in.

'*Taip*!' she cried out. Her only words during our lovemaking.

Later, between the sheets, relaxing, quietly recording every minute of the fuck at the back of my mind, enjoying her soft presence next to me, absorbing her smell and warmth, it felt so comfortable. She felt the same.

'Do you believe in reincarnation?' Aida asked.

'Actually, no,' I replied. I was not one for mumbo jumbo or new age claptrap. 'Why?'

'It felt as if we knew each other already, you know, some time before. It was so easy, so natural,' she said.

'I don't think so,' I objected gently.

Hinting she's been with a lot of men before.

This is how I discovered I was only the fifth man she had had sex with. It didn't feel that way. She had a great natural talent for fucking, it seemed to me.

Aida's story: the first was a Belgian who was on holiday in Lithuania; they'd become friendly but no more and had begun to correspond and some months later he had out of the blue invited her to go on a Christmas holiday with her. They had met up in London where she'd given up her virginity to him in a small Bloomsbury hotel, and the next day they had taken a charter flight to a Thailand beach where they had alternated sunbathing and fucking for a whole fortnight. She now said she hadn't particularly enjoyed it or him, but had felt obliged as he had paid so much money to fly her there and pay for the holiday. Had apparently given up his job and savings to organise the trip. Never again, she decided on her return, would she feel obliged to have sex with a man because he was entertaining her or spending money on her. Six months later in Vilnius, there had been a one-night stand with a Pole. She had been very drunk and he had been very rough was all she said. (Later, in the morning, I discovered he had forced her to have anal sex and she was deeply ashamed to admit she had enjoyed a particularly strong come as result.) The following summer she had saved up enough to travel in Europe, and met up with the Belgian man in Holland but had somehow ended up sleeping with a friend of his, a Dutch man. She never returned to Lithuania when he asked her to live with him. She'd become pregnant and had a termination. The dreams that ensued had been awful and the second time she had found herself pregnant, she was determined to have the child. But by then, the relationship with her Dutch lover, a boat builder, was already deteriorating.

The little boy was born and she stopped sleeping with Marcel, even though they still had to share the same bed. While nursing the baby, she found out how to surf the Internet on his computer and discovered the chat rooms. Thus the Swiss episode. They met for a night at the Krasnapolsky Hotel off the Dam when he came to Amsterdam. He invited her to Switzerland with the baby. She went. He insisted she shave her genitals and also wanted anal sex. She quickly realised he was not right and returned to Holland with her tail between her legs and begged her Dutch ex's forgiveness. Which he granted, after all they still had the little boy in common. Which brought me up to date.

It was midnight on my watch. I had become hard again.

We fucked. Missionary position this time, so I could see her wide blue eyes implore me with a thousand silent words as I moved in and out of her and wiped stray hairs away from her hot forehead. That look just killed me, I knew. One I would find it hard to ever forget. Damn her. Why couldn't she come with her eyes closed as most do. She came, I didn't. Grew soft again. She had said nothing when I thrust myself inside her with no protection. She rang home on her mobile, informing whoever that she was not returning that night. We fell asleep.

Morning came and I was aching all over. She still slept peacefully. I moved the cover away from her body and parted her legs. She still dripped my seed between her thick lower lips and I buried my tongue in her cunt and woke her with repeated assaults of lust. Her eyes still shone like beacons.

I shaved as she lazed around. Had to tell her I had a series of meetings that morning. We crossed the canal for breakfast in a café. She had a croissant with thin slices of cheese and ham and a mug of hot chocolate. I watched her eat. Sex gave her a wonderful glow. She had a train back to her village on every half hour so was in no hurry. She was not expected at the chocolate factory today anyway. There was a small record shop opening right then, shutters being pulled aside, across the narrow street from the café. She shyly asked if we had time to look inside. We had.

Aida had atrocious taste in music by my standards. I bought her the new Metallica double-CD and one of operatic arias she had heard of on a commercial for margarine which had featured a catchy tune from Delibes' Lakme. She was delighted. I gave her my business card and noted her address and mobile number. I walked her to Central Station where we parted quietly. To my relief, she was not into emotional good-byes. Neither was I and I was glad to be spared further words. My vocabulary and mood was just not up to it this morning. It reminded me of so many other early mornings or late night separations and trains to marital beds that still wrenched my insides into sharp, jagged pieces.

Hank Van der Meer was waiting for me between the philosophy and anthropology sections of the Athenaeum bookshop. A gangly man with a shock of red, curly hair and John Lennon glasses who could only have been an academic or a book dealer. He was both.

He took me to a drugs bar nearby where he ordered an absinthe, while I stuck to my usual soft drink.

I introduced myself as a journalist preparing an article on the more clandestine aspects of book collecting, suggesting he had been recommended to me at a London auction house by someone whose name I wasn't allowed to mention. Actually, his name often appeared on my web searches when it came to rare books whose provenance was often shaded in irregularities. In civilian life, Van der Meer taught the history of book publishing at a special book trade school here in Amsterdam.

Without specifically identifying the Le Carré book, I described the circumstances surrounding its origin and asked him what would be the best way to either acquire or dispose of such a choice item.

It was like pushing a button or clicking on the computer's 'search' button and I frantically tried to keep up with the rapid pace of Van der Meer's pontifications, jotting down all the names on my legal pad. Many I had come across before during the course of my initial search, but I noted them anyway. But there were also new names and places. He ordered another drink and became more conspiratorial, and showered me with tales of bibliophilia galore. Scams, crooks, forgeries, desperate collectors, shady book scouts and runners, legendary operators.

I asked him about likely purchasers of the book, if it came on the market. This set the Dutch academic thinking.

Actually, he couldn't see the book appealing to more than a handful of private collectors. Now, university libraries, that was another thing altogether. The item I described was a curiosity, after all. An anomaly. And most genuine collectors specialised in specific authors, publishers or subjects. There were a few mavericks he could think of in Texas and California. Then there was some woman in New York, Cornelis something or other, who was always on the look-out for extraordinary items in the field of modern firsts, but she was a bit of a mystery in the trade. Was never seen at auctions and only worked through a handful of dealers. A bit of a legend, really.

I wrote all this down, like a real journalist, paid for the drinks, thanked him.

My next meeting was soon upon me. A more dubious underworld contact who had the lowdown on smuggling rare items across borders. We met outside the American Discount Centre on Kalverstraat. As arranged, I carried a copy of the *Financial Times* under my arms. He acknowledged my presence and I followed him down the street. He preferred to talk while we walked, spurned my suggestion we sit for a coffee or a drink. He seemed to look at me with much suspicion and was taken aback that all I wanted to talk about was books. He provided some information, but I wasn't making much progress truly. Some of the same names kept on popping up in the conversation. A rich collector in Texas whose name he didn't know and was into both stolen paintings as well as rare books. I asked him about Cornelis and a deep frown crossed his forehead. 'You mean Cornelia?' he asked.

'Maybe,' I answered.

'If I were you I would steer clear,' he suggested. 'That woman is trouble.'

But, when pressed, he had never met her. It was all just hearsay. Some broad in New York with a serious reputation, who was heavily into book collecting. He agreed to make a phone call and arranged for me to meet up with another source that afternoon. I thanked him.

I had a couple of hours to spare before the next meeting and walked briskly among the Amsterdam traffic, along canals and tram lines. All the time, I could still smell Aida and the touch of her lips all over me. By now, she must be back in her village, playing with her baby. I hoped she didn't get round to putting that ad in the newspaper and sell herself cheaply to some man with money who would only use her. 'Willing to be a Mistress'? 'Will fuck for apartment and roof over my head. Anal optional.'? 'Hot Russian girl seeks Sugar Daddy'?

The following meeting came to nothing. The small bald man in his Gestapo-like leather coat and clumpy shoes had a poor grasp of English and knew nothing about the unscrupulous side of the book world. I tried the Poshard name out on him and drew a blank.

I had open reservations on a series of flights back to London and decided to catch the first one. As contingency, the hotel room was booked for a further night, but I hadn't expected to sleep over another night. At the reception desk, they couldn't find my key. Suggested I maybe go to the room, as the maid might still be up there.

The door wasn't locked. Expecting a Surinam matron busily airing out the bed sheets and no doubt sniffing disapprovingly all the excesses of the night before, I innocently walked in. Trust a British detective to not know the rules of the game. As I stepped into the room and closed the door, there was a soft, muted shuffle of feet behind me and I felt a massive blow to the back of my head.

It all went dark.

5: Cornelia

It had been some months now since Cornelia's last contract and she was getting restless.

There had been empty, sleepless nights. With no passing man or woman to appease the boredom of loneliness. She knew there was something missing in her life. Her heart was untouched, guiltless in the face of all the horrors she had witnessed and the murders she had committed.

There were days when she lost herself in her dance, content to swim along to the rhythm and flow of the music, impervious to the envious gaze of men touching themselves in the darkness or fantasising wildly at the sight of her unclad body. She was of late spending a small fortune on CD's and spent hours putting together new compilations of songs which she changed every week to strip to. But the pleasure of the mindless declination of music and body movements never supplied her with more than temporary release.

Her heart was still as cold as stone. Cornelia knew this would never change. It was the way she was made and she had no time for regrets. There had been hurt on the rare occasions when she had allowed herself to experience feelings, whether as a child or as fully grown woman, and she felt no need to repeat the bad experiences. She had to make do with what was left. Her books, the wonder of a melody that could reach down deep inside her, a pleasant meal, the smells of Manhattan on a spring day, the satisfaction of a kill cleanly executed, the feel of the wind on her cheek as she raced up Broadway towards the Strand early on a Monday morning to peruse new arrivals with a nice twinge of expectation. But small pleasures were not enough to appease the hole inside that seemed to be growing at an exponential rate.

Someone had once remarked to her that there was just too much beauty in the world, but Cornelia was blind to it. And the fact just made her damn angry.

It also worried her, as the state of boredom settled intangibly over her life, that she missed the thrill of the chase and kill.

The blood lust.

So, for the first time ever, there being no new book she was in desperate need of, and with her checking account still in relatively healthy shape, Cornelia phoned her contact number and made herself available for an assignment.

There was always work for a trained assasin.

It was just a question of waiting, now.

She took a deep breath as she replaced the receiver, realising she had taken a brand new step in a whole different direction. She knew it had been a mistake within minutes, but her pride prevented her from calling back and cancelling her request.

She took a cold shower.

She had been stupid.

What next?

A notch by her tattoo for every new kill? In ink or by scar?

Stupid, stupid girl!

'Getting a liking for it, are you now my dear?'

She knew there was no point pretending. The voice at the other end of the line knew more about her than she did herself. She had long suspected he, or they, even kept an occasional watch on her. Caution was understandable. But she feigned surprise.

'What do you mean?'

'You still haven't read the books you acquired last time

around. And you're sitting on a tidy pile of cash. You could even give up the dancing for, say, a year and live on your savings.'

'So?' Cornelia retorted.

'So, I have a job for you,' was all he said, not rising to her bait.

'Good.'

'But you will have to be patient. The target is not yet in the country, but we have solid evidence she will be arriving soon.'

'A woman?'

'Yes. You've never objected in the past. Female solidarity and all that!' There was a dark streak of irony in his voice.

'It's not a problem. Never has been,' Cornelia answered.

'Fine.'

'I'll be on standby, then.'

'Excellent. Usual fee?'

'No problem.'

'Good girl. And, tell you what…'

'Yes?' Cornelia queried.

'Maybe you could vary your stage moves. Devise something a little different while you're waiting for the call. I think your boredom is showing in your set; you've become a little mechanical, my dear.'

So, he came to watch her, it appeared. Cornelia shivered. She was about to ask him more, but the phone went dead as her interlocutor hung up.

Receiver still cradled between shoulder and ear, Cornelia wondered about him. Which face in the audience was he? Which goggle-eyed anonymous spectator? Did he wear glasses? Did she excite him sexually? She had a posse of regulars; some came, some went, it was difficult to keep track of them all in the blurry darkness that surrounded the stages on which she performed, and anyway she never did give much thought to the men who lapped up her every indecent move.

She smiled: maybe he had even liked the tattoo. She put the phone down. Her heart suddenly felt lighter.

She helped herself to an apple from the refrigerator and, greedily munching through it, began to sort out her latest pile of CD's. So he felt she needed to put some variety in her act, did he? So be it. She would need a new set of songs then. Special tunes indeed.

It took her the whole afternoon to make her mind up. Switching and changing endlessly between the tunes that had recently caught her fancy. Not all could be danced to, she knew, as she assayed tentative steps barefoot on the thick rug of her front room to the new songs. Back and forth she moved from the improvised dance floor to the compact Aiwa hi-fi, recording, erasing and recording again until she was satisfied by her new sequence.

It began with Bruce Springsteen's 'Lift Me Up', a tune she had first heard over the closing credits of the John Sayles movie *Limbo*, and which was the only decent thing on the soundtrack CD. It was a melody that just chilled her to the bone, Springsteen at his most melancholy falsetto with a surging wall of synthesised strings rising behind the plaintive call for love and help. This she would dance to with her eyes shut. The song demanded it. She stripped down to her underwear and practised her moves, tentative at first but soon growing in assurance until every chord paralleled a flexing sinew.

She followed this with the Walkabouts' 'Crime Story'.

And for her finale, after much experimentation, Cornelia at last settled on another haunting melody, also from a movie soundtrack, a short Scott Walker song from *Pola X*, which she had to replay in a loop so it would be long enough to dance to.

New moves he wanted, new moves he would get.

So what if the music was a touch plaintive? The clubs

always complained about her left-of-field choices. Asked her for more cheerful, upbeat tunes. As if the paying customers cared as long as they caught sight of her tits and pussy. But she always told them she came as package, the music and her. No negotiations.

What did they expect her to dance to? 'Big Spender' or 'Gentlemen Prefer Blondes'? Damn it, a girl had to retain some sort of integrity if she was displaying her wide open cunt to any punter willing to part with as little as five dollars for a watered-down beer.

'What the fuck was that exhibition all about?' Ade was crimson with rage as he faced Cornelia in the makeshift dressing room she shared with the other girls on duty today.

'OK, so it was a bit more raunchy than usual,' she replied, wiping the sweat from her body with the green flannel towel she always brought along in her bag. None of the other workers here used green towels. Gave her a feeling of safer hygiene. She hated the place's antediluvian shower stalls and always avoided using them. She'd wait until she returned to the apartment before taking a cleansing bubble bath to wash away the sin and sweat. 'Aren't you always begging me to be more upbeat?'

'Upbeat? Raunchier?' Ade sputtered. 'Couldn't you see what you were up to, Cornelia? It just wasn't like you... Fingers everywhere, those bends... You'll have the place closed down. You don't realise.'

'Come on...' she tried to counter his protests. 'I've seen some of the other girls get up to much worse.'

'Not here you haven't, Cornelia. We offer exotic dancing, titillation, not hardcore pornography, gal. There are definitely limits. Even here.'

'Don't go overboard, Ade.'

'What got into you, anyway?' he asked.

'Let's say there was a good friend in the audience, and I wanted to give a show to remember. OK?'

He downed his glass of vermouth.

'I didn't notice anyone special out there. Seemed the usual crowd. Although some of them seemed to be going somewhat red in the face.'

'So,' Cornelia volunteered, 'They will all make return visits...'

'I have no doubt about that, Cornelia. But I'm afraid that if you pull that stunt again, you're out of here on your fanny. I know you have friends in... how shall I put it, interesting places, but I'll have no choice. I'm not about to endanger our license.'

Cornelia threw her towel on the bench and slipped her T-shirt on. Ade stared at her nudity. There were two types of women, he knew, those who began the process of dressing with knickers and those who started with the brassière. He had never drawn any ontological conclusions from this choice but always suspected those who covered their top first, leaving their cunt and ass in full view must be hotter than hot in bed. Which left Cornelia, who never wore a bra in civilian life. He'd always wondered about her sex life.

As she dressed, she asked him:

'But did you like the music, Ade?'

He shrugged, turned his back on her to leave the dressing room.

'The music stank... But you were sensational. You were too good for them or any spy from the Giuliani clean-up brigade.'

'Thanks, Ade,' she shouted back at him over the sound of the honky tonk music to which the next dancer, a plump black girl with her share of silicon, was stripping to on stage.

'But,' he reminded her, 'Tonight's was a one-off performance. Comprende?'

'Spoilsport,' she mumbled and slipped on her jeans.

'I heard that,' he shouted back at her.

She gathered her stage clothes and make-up and stuffed the lot into a tote bag. Moments later, she walked out onto Madison. It was approaching midnight, the evening wind had died away and the air was unusually cool and clear. She walked down in the direction of the West Village. She needed to clear her head and thoughts and forsook her usual cab. On Sixth she reached the large Barnes and Noble down by Twenty-third Street. It was still open and she walked in. There was not enough time until closing to explore the new fiction section and she lingered by the magazines.

She leafed aimlessly through a handful of women's magazines, then moved on to the health and cookery rack. Across from it a lanky teenager in baggy jeans and black leather jacket looked up at her and put down the magazine he had been reading, a furtive look on his face. A skin mag, Cornelia noticed out of the corner of her eye.

She smiled at him.

Didn't they say in all the lifestyle magazines that book superstores were the new pick-up places for young professionals?

'Hi,' she greeted the stranger.

Looked him up and down. No pimples. Clean shaven at least. He would do. Right now, the load felt heavy and she didn't want to spend the night alone.

'Hello,' he tentatively replied.

'The place is closing in a few minutes,' she pointed out.

'I know,' he stuttered.

She went up to him.

'I'm Corrie,' she said.

'Jay.'

'So, Jay, do you have any plans?'

'Not really,' he answered, shuffling his feet.

'Listen,' she said to him. 'I won't beat about the bush: I'm damn lonely and want company tonight. And seeing you standing here at this time of night, I assume you're lonely too.'

He reluctantly nodded in agreement.

'Care to be lonely together?' She ventured a hand towards him.

A burly security guard by the store's main door announced closing time, distracting his attention.

For an instant, Cornelia panicked. It occurred to her she hadn't yet had her post-dance bath, and a thin cake of sweat no doubt still enveloped the geography of her skin. Further, she had totally forgotten to wash her fingers, and she remembered acutely how, during the course of the new set, she had aggressively fingered herself in the heat of the action. And that she had been wet, at the thought of the owner of the voice at the other end of the line being in the audience.

She abhorred vulgarity. Surely, making a pass at this young man was the height of irresponsibility? Why not push her fingers under his nose and ask him to sniff. 'Here, this is me, this is my cunt, this is the unsheer fragrance of my despair! Smell, smell me, damn you!'

She fell back to earth.

The young guy, surely he couldn't be older than twenty or so, shot her another nervous glance.

Then, 'Maybe not,' he said. 'It's a bit too... sudden, you know what I mean...'

But still he didn't move.

What was it with him? Cornelia thought. Maybe my boobs aren't voluptuous enough, my hair isn't teased, I don't dress like a stripper should? Thinks I'm just another student with a head full of complexes, too much trouble to handle. Or he's too good for me? Or I'm too good for him? Bet he'd get hard soon if I only told him I'm shaven below. They all love that. Men.

She seethed.

But she kept her calm.

'A romantic, I see,' she joked.

The boy blushed and made for the store door.

Cornelia walked home, taking a shortcut through Washington Square.

She just didn't understand. She had offered her body and he'd wanted her heart too. The affectional greed of men would never cease to surprise her.

She spent the night with a good thriller and rock music blaring out at maximum volume on her headphones. And a long soak in her bath tub, contemplating the deformed image of her crotch through the vacillating green water. The tattoo stared at her and she contemplated making it disappear by growing her pubic thatch back. But decided against it.

She returned to her own innocuous dance routine, to Ade's great relief. The guys in the audience had become a tad restless on some days; maybe her legend had grown by word of mouth since her notorious session and they now expected more. She even added a big band tune to her tape and took a tip from Anita, the Italian girl from Milan who taught her how to do a headstand with her legs indecently wide apart but just out of the punters' view. The stunt drew a few extra tips, but was hell on her wrists.

She found several new work outfits at Religious Sex on St Mark's Place. One in shiny black leather, evoking tantalising echoes of S&M. Another was of wonderful see-through silk and even came with matching stockings and garter belts. She also experimented on a couple of occasions with cans of liquid latex which she sprayed on to herself in the changing room like a second skin and later gradually peeled off as her set progressed. But it proved too painful and also lacked elegance when a whole area would sometimes tear at an inopportune moment or in the wrong place. It also made her itch afterwards and a striptease artist with visible pimples and sores would just not do, she knew.

Cornelia waited for the call but it was unusually slow in coming.

She killed time as best she could.

She even timed a whole day to fit in five movies in quick succession, dashing between the floors and screens of the Union Square multiplex. By the end, she couldn't even remember a single incident from the first late morning film.

And the pager she carried in her purse stayed silent.

She even contemplated getting round to read all of Proust or making a start on the books by Tolstoy or Dostoevsky she had always relegated to later times.

The weather invisibly warmed and she switched from jeans to a light flannel dress she always wore around Easter time. Gee, another ritual. Was she becoming an old spinster with a sackful of habits? Better keep a sense of humour about it all, she reckoned.

One of the few girls from the club with whom she had a tentative friendship came down with the flu and asked her if she could help out by taking over her slots at another joint up East Side. Cornelia agreed. It was a club she had never danced at. Had a dodgy reputation. At any rate, it was only for three days. When the management insisted she conform and follow her set by offering lap and table dances, she didn't resist. A rough crowd, and she grew tired of all the roving hands she had to smack down every time they tried it on. Which only seemed to encourage the guys further. The one working girl, the strange one, the pretentious one who thought she was better than all the others and refused to put out. There was a queue for her when she vacated the stage.

So she lap danced.

So she table danced, their bad breath swirling across her

bare flesh as she undulated, the stale smell of tobacco assaulting her senses.

'Come on…'

'Wider, babe…'

'A nice present if you join me in the john…'

'Don't be so precious, it's only a hand…'

'An eenie-weenie finger…'

'That's what I call a pussy, girl. Would love to fist you…'

'Just a blow job, swear it won't hurt…'

'Tell me, do you like it up the ass, sweetie? You'd love it…'

She was tired, pissed, her calf muscles hurt. This was her
last day here and the final lap dance. The guy was just a
cipher, some anonymous executive in a grey three-piece suit.
Not a talker, at least. He sat on the chair while Cornelia
paraded in front of him, dancing, flexing her extremities,
opening herself for his perusal. Cupping her slight tits and
teasing her resolutely unaroused nipples for his delectation.
Watching him mentally drool. A damp back room at the
club.

She watched the seconds slowly tick away on the clock on
the wall. One minute to go. He'd only paid for five. Time to
assume her final position in the rigmarole. She retreated from
him, took a step back, turned so that the man was now gazing
at her back, the regal whiteness of her backside. Walked back
towards the seated man, her hips still swaying gently to the
sound of the music in the club on the other side of the wall.
Reaching him, Cornelia squatted down and sat herself on his
knees. He was hard. Of course. It was too much not to expect.
She resumed her swaying, slowly grinding her arse against his
lap. Glanced at the clock. Only a few seconds to go. Wouldn't
have time to come. Some did, she always knew when, felt the
heat through the layers of their garments and the sudden soft-
ening of the cock, or the electric pulse that coursed through
their body as she rubbed against them. She could hear him

breathe. Peppermint gum. Suddenly she felt his hands roughly circle her and grab her breasts.

'No hands,' she screamed over the loudness of the music.

'Oh...' he meekly protested, but didn't take his hands away, painfully kneading her nipples.

'You know the fucking rules...' she told him, and deliberately peed all over his lap. Damn, he had it coming! They all did and he was paying the price. And stepped off him and out of the private room.

'JESUS!' he cried out as Cornelia disappeared. The circular stain of her urine fast spreading across the greyness of his trousers.

She knew he wouldn't have the guts to lodge a protest. And wondered mischievously how he would explain the stain to his wife. He'd been wearing a wedding ring. Most of the private customers did.

Cornelia was washing her smalls in the bathroom sink when the call came.

'Sorry it's been so long, my dear.'

'It has,' she said. 'Problems?'

'Circumstances,' he said.

'I see.'

She felt like asking him whether he had attended 'the' performance, but resolved not to bring the subject of her dancing up unless he did so first.

'The target arrives in the country tomorrow. On the way to New Orleans.'

'The famed Big Easy,' Cornelia said. 'I've always wanted to go there.'

'Now's your chance, my dear,' he answered. 'You'll have to make the hit locally. The target has a plane connection in Chicago, but I would never advise working in airports. Too dangerous, a recipe for all sorts of disasters.'

'I understand.'

'Local arrangements will be made for you.'

'Good.'

This meant she wouldn't have to travel carrying obvious weapons. They would be made available to her on arrival in New Orleans. The Organisation's planning had never let her down. So far.

That evening, she picked up the customary dossier. The woman was indeed pretty. The details provided about her were few, but Cornelia also knew that the less she knew the better. Tomorrow's flight to New Orleans made a connection in Chicago and would arrive early evening. Arrangements had been made for her cover in the form of a short-term contract with a local club. There was no need to stretch credibility, after all.

She added a bunch of dance tapes and a couple of flimsy work outfits to the luggage she had already prepared that afternoon.

Like every night before an assignment, Cornelia slept badly. She moved and stirred but it wasn't her habitual sense of heightened expectancy. She was aware it was not a case of nerves either, no, it was something else. After all the waiting, there was a deep sense of lassitude within her. A tiredness she had never felt before.

Maybe her life had reached a crossroads.

And changes would have to be made.

But where? And how?

As the plane banked over Lake Pontchartrain in its downward approach to the airport, Cornelia in her window seat barely noted the landscape beneath, lost in a daydream of roads not taken and a twisted labyrinth of memory.

She had by now convinced herself this would be the last job she accepted. A final hit for the road, so to speak. A clean-cut elimination to keep her record unblemished. Maybe she would travel. Warmer climes, beaches, somewhere her heart might benefit from the sun and lose its natural coldness. Make her more human. Normal. Maybe one day it could be the white picket fences. But deep inside, she knew she was just fooling herself.

The fasten seat belts announcement shook her out of her reverie. She brought her seat upright before the attendant could chide her for not doing. The aircraft landed with an imperceptible bump and, for yet another time, she memorised her dossier. The address of the club, the small hotel she would be staying at a few blocks from the notorious Bourbon Street, the telephone numbers she had to rely on – one for a suitable weapon, another in case of emergency, and yet another for legal advice if all else failed.

The overhead light was switched off and, in unison, half the passengers rose from their seats and began gathering their bags from the overhead compartments. Cornelia lingered in her seat. She had no wish to wrestle her way out of the plane and knew she would overtake most of the hurrying passengers on the concourse; she had longer legs.

The heat and the humidity hit her full in the face as she exited the airport building. She took a deep breath of air. Yes, she was going to like the place, she could feel it in her bones.

She caught a cab to the city and banished all her confused thoughts to the depths of her memory. This was now Louisiana time. Cornelia switched to work mode.

Here I come, Miss Poshard. Your angel of death.

6: Martin

I opened my eyes.
I was no longer in the room.
Amsterdam, stranded.

I was a captive of my own nightmares, full of the floating grace of women's bodies. Kay's pallid languor, Aida's darker, more sensual, supple limbs flaying, mouths, shifting configurations of wide-open lips shaped for an obscene blessing of my cock. Moles, beauty stains roaming at liberty over the geography of their skins. A nipple there. Kay, Aida, Catherine, Lisa, Jasmine, Evelyn, Montana, whose? As soon as I focused on one curve or an orifice, the view changed and the landscape merged into a tangle of crumpled sheets.

In the epicentre of the darkness where I hung, a body without a body, there were eyes. Brown, pleading; pale blue, begging; green, inviting like a tropical lagoon; grey, hard and resentful.

I closed my eyes, beckoning the darkness back.

A bright light shone against my retina. And again the spectacle of naked bodies, long legs that went on forever, a midnight choir of sheer unadulterated desire.

And the blood.

And the silence.

And the shocking vision of Kay in a bed of blood, her eyes hanging on to consciousness, drowning in anger, in surprise, and the scalpel flying through the air and ravaging the virgin snow of her uncovered skin. Like a silent movie, every gesture in exaggerated slow motion as if it wasn't real, just a stylised version of life. And death.

I recognised the dream that had been pursuing me for
weeks now and I realised there was just no running away. I
was in an Amsterdam hotel room and lay unconscious,
immobilised in the handcuffs of my torment. And here I was
to linger forever, my own version of hell, the lower circle of
my infamy, the punishment for my past betrayals. I cried.
Without making a sound, or shedding a real tear. Ever the liar.

On and on and on and on.

Finally, I emerged from my purgatory and my first thought
as I broke out of the zone of darkness was: what possibly had
I done wrong? The cases I took on were never dangerous:
missing wives, sisters or books. Which seldom called for violence.

I shook my head and got to my knees. The bedside lamp
was on. I was now alone in the room. My aggressor hadn't
stuck around. I looked at my watch. It was still there; the
most expensive item on me, so that ruled out an opportunist
thief, I reckoned. I'd only been under for ten minutes at most,
it seemed. I looked back. The door to the room was now
closed. I saw the key on the bed and my emptied Samsonite
and all its contents strewn across the thin carpet.

I washed my face with cold water and finally regained all
my senses. Swept my fingers across the back of my head: the
bump was already fading. I'd live. Maybe have a bad
headache later.

I tidied up the contents of my case. At first, there didn't
appear to be anything missing. My notes on the Poshard case
were still in the inside pocket of the jacket I had been wearing
all day and the intruder hadn't thought of frisking me after I'd
fallen down. Possibly worried that the noise might attract
someone to the room he had flown the coop, almost straight-
away. But it didn't make sense. If I'd come across an
opportunist thief, he would have taken my laptop, my passport, my wallet or the Tag Heuer. But they had all been spared.

Then I realised the manila envelope with Christopher Streetfield's notes and the photographs of his wife was missing.

A shiver ran down my spine.

No, it didn't make the slightest sense.

It was the wrong case.

Or a warning that I was stepping on the wrong toes.

But whose?

Naturally, at the hotel desk they knew nothing, hadn't noticed anyone suspicious inquiring about me. I made no fuss and settled my bill and took a cab to Schipol airport where I caught the first available flight back to Stansted.

Strong gusts of wind swirling down from the coast were assaulting the airport runways and the flight was delayed for an hour. I rang Aida.

Her voice was wonderfully chirpy.

'Aida here.'

'Hi, it's me.'

'It's so nice to hear from you.'

'You got back safely?'

'Yes. I got caught in the rain while I biked back to the cottage, but it was a nice feeling. But my ex was very unhappy I stayed out all night, you know. He knew from my shiny eyes. I can't hide what I've been doing. Sex. He got very angry. Sometimes he scares me. I really have to find somewhere to live on my own, well, with my little boy.'

'I'm sorry about that. Listen, Aida, I'm at Schipol. Just wanted to say how much I enjoyed yesterday night. I felt comfortable with you. It was nice. Really.'

'Me too.'

'I have some travelling to do, but I'd like to see you again. I don't know when. One day.'

'Yes,' she said, with no hint of emotion.

'You'd like that too?'

'Yes. I'll never forget the way you kiss. You're a treasure,' the young Lithuanian woman said, aiming an arrow straight at my heart.

'Really?'

'Yes, the treasure in my collection.'

'Your collection? Makes it sound as if I'm just another cock in your zoo of men...'

'No,' Aida said. 'I told you, you're my fifth.'

I still didn't know whether I should believe her. But I wanted to.

'I'm flattered to be listed as a treasure, then. Highly flattered.'

There was an announcement on the departure lounge tannoy.

'I have to go, Aida. I'll stay in touch.'

'Yes.'

The taxi driver took the Midtown Tunnel route in from Kennedy and it was New York.

Again.

Manhattan. That island of lost souls. So many times before, my search for missing spouses had brought me here. As if such a small island, however jampacked with bodies, could ever be a perfect hiding place, a refuge for hearts on the run, a sanctuary from a past that hurt too much. Maybe the anonymity of its deep canyons lined with skyscrapers, its frantic pace and cacophony of languages and cheap trainer shops on every damn corner?

Before leaving London, I'd called Streetfield and told him I had a lead on his wife and had to go to New York to follow it up. He seemed to accept the news with no surprise, as if nothing would ever catch him wrong-footed again. He sounded low, about to give up on her forever, I felt. Which suited me, of course. Didn't even enquire what sort of extra costs my trip to the US would provoke. I didn't ask him for new photos to replace the ones stolen in Amsterdam. I had no need for them.

I lowered the cab window to escape the unbearable fumes as the car plunged into the tunnel after the inevitable traffic jam leading up to it.

My hotel was off Washington Square and I quickly unloaded my case, connected the laptop to the awkward slot under the telephone set, checked for e-mails and slumped down on the bed for a few hours to fight the insidious effect of the jet-lag. I never can sleep on planes.

The doze was dream-free for a change.

My New York contact man had no name; he preferred it that way. In my mind, and in my occasional notes, he was just John Doe. The name he'd once suggested when I insisted on some form of identification in our communications.

We met for a meal at Veselka, a Ukrainian restaurant on Second Avenue. I provided him with the names I'd so far harvested in my quest for the younger Poshard sister, and asked for the skinny on crooked book dealers, here and across America. I also mentioned Cornelia.

Doe's eyes clouded over.

'Yes, I know Cornelia,' he answered, sipping on his cup of borscht.

'What's the connection?'

'I'm not sure,' I answered.

'She's bad news. Freelance, but trouble by all accounts. But you might be barking down the wrong avenue. She's not a gal who gets involved with missing people. Quite the contrary. Better known making people disappear. Permanently. Or so the rumour goes.'

'Actually, her name cropped up with regards to the rare book connection.'

'Doesn't make sense to me,' John Doe said.

'Forget Cornelia, then. What else can you tell me?'

A Polish waitress with sultry lips brought my dish of pierogi.

'The Poshard girl has been in town. A few weeks ago. But no one knows where she is now. Might already have left.'

'How do you know that?' I asked him.

'Reliable sources.'

Apparently, she had stayed at the Algonquin Hotel. Had seldom left her room. There was a man with her, though. Much older than her, middle-aged, upper-class, could have been her father, someone from the hotel had said. But Doe couldn't get a more precise description of the man who'd been with Louise.

At least, this gave me something to go on from here.

We finished our coffees. Silence settled between us.

'And the sister, Nola, arrived in town this morning,' John Doe then said.

Curiouser and curiouser.

Something inside was ringing alarm bells and telling me that the damn rare book was just an excuse, that Nola Poshard had little interest in retrieving it. Hmmm.

'Where is she staying?' I asked.

'Also at the Algonquin. The Poshard family always stay there, it appears.'

'That's on Forty-fourth Street, isn't it?'

'Yes, east of Times Square and Fifth.'

'Maybe I should visit.'

'Perhaps you should.' There was the hint of a smile drawn across his gaunt features.

McNelson Sheldon inspired little confidence and I could imagine the shiver of disgust coursing through the spines of all the books he handled as they passed between his hands. A repulsive little sod. We'd met in the Rare Book room at the

Strand, on Broadway. It was now mid-afternoon and I felt I
was on a wild goose chase.

But Sheldon had actually heard of the book. It wasn't
apocryphal. Apparently, one copy had been auctioned in
Texas a few months before, long before its disappearance
from the Poshard collection, so there must more than one of
these unauthorised proofs in existence. The slimy dealer
passed his tongue over his dry lips and informed me that the
book had gone for over ten thousand bucks.

'A quite unique item,' he added. ' So many rich collectors
in Texas with more money than acumen, I reckon.'

I asked him about Cornelia.

'A bright one, she is,' he smiled broadly. 'She doesn't only
collect. She also reads the books. Interesting criteria. Very
idiosyncratic.' She was a good customer of his. I asked how I
could get in touch with her.

'The Le Carré proof is just not her type of book,' Sheldon
insisted. 'Not at all.'

'I'd still like to talk to her,' I added.

'Elusive lady,' he pointed out. 'She always makes the
contact, not me.'

I managed to extract her PO box number at Cooper
Station from him. That was all he could give me.

Why did I feel I needed a thorough shower after I'd parted
with the pockmarked dealer?

I settled down at my Washington Square Place hotel, now
ready for a proper night's sleep. Out of habit I booted up the
laptop. I had mail. It was my Wandsworth computer magi-
cian to whom I'd passed on the Poshard sister's stolen hard
drive. It appears it had been deliberately wiped clean barely a
week ago. I checked my diary. The day before Nola Poshard
came to me with the case. However, he had managed to
retrieve a single document file whose ghost somehow hadn't
deserted the computer's cavernous memory and had been sent

as an attachment to an e-mail to Louise Poshard on the very day I assumed her sister had tried to eliminate any evidence. He was sending it along, as a text file. It was big at over 20k, but anything Nola had tried to hide from me must have some significance.

I clicked to open the salvaged file. At first, it wouldn't work so I had to reconfigure things a little. A task that always made me nervous. Finally, the screen on my laptop filled with words. A story. A life.

First came a note, a letter:

My sweet Louise,
Thanks for New York. It was everything I expected and more. We agreed not to talk further about our situation, but all I can do is feel revulsion about the hold Nola has over you. I am a writer. I write. For what it's worth, I felt strangely compelled to write down our story. I hope you recognise it, that I have not been too melodramatic. One day I hope you understand why I have written about us this way.
Will I ever see you again? After that house in New Orleans.
A tender kiss and a desperate hug.

There was no name or signature.

Fiction? Reality?
That night in New York I could find no answers in my mind after reading Louise's tale.

THE SILENCE THAT STANDS
BETWEEN THE WORDS

7: A Hotel Room Fuck (or The Story of Louise)

How they first met is unimportant.
Or, at any rate, another story altogether.
A different one.

Actually, it was in an Internet chat room.

Here, they both arrive at Kennedy Airport on different flights from Europe, barely one hour and two terminals apart. Initially the flight she had suggested taking was bound for Newark and cheaper, but he had been unable to coordinate his own travel arrangements to match hers.

After retrieving his case from the luggage delivery area and verifying her flight details, he kills time wandering through the busy, rundown hallways and alleyways of the building cluttered with passengers in various forms of transit. Idly wandering what she might actually look like. Checks out the stroke magazines in the Hudson News concession. There's a new one he's never come across before, called *Barely Legal*. He nervously glances aside as he leafs through it. Time passes slowly. A double cheeseburger and fries and a large coke take up another ten minutes.

He finally makes his way toward the terminal where the Virgin Airways flights disembark, dragging his own case behind him on its dodgy wheels. A screen announces the arrival of her plane. She must now be queuing at passport control. He finds a seat to the right of the luggage pick-up area from which vantage point he will see all the passengers emerging through the corridor from immigration. He holds his breath one moment. Suddenly, the whole thing doesn't sound so wise after all. What if, what if?

The Gatwick flight crowd streams through the corridor. So many of them, the plane must have been quite full. Saunter down the short flight of stairs towards the luggage carousels.

She is among the last to emerge. A dozen times already he has convinced himself she isn't on the plane. Had been playing a game with him all the time. Had missed the flight by barely a minute or so back in Europe. Had been discovered by her Masters and held back in captivity. Had come to her senses and realised this whole New York thing was quite pointless after all.

Finally, a slip of a girl with luminous features makes her way past the security guard posted at the top the short flight of stairs and tiptoes her way down, concertina'd almost by two burly six-footed businessmen in charcoal-coloured suits and matching attaché-cases. Her dark blue skirt is short, swirls around her knees. Her T-shirt is white, its thin material clinging to her skin. Even from where he sits he can see the outline of her nipples through it, or is it the rings?

Jesus, she is so young!

But he knew that already, didn't he?

As she reaches the bottom of the stairs and her involuntary escorts scatter in different directions, she looks around the luggage enclosure, seeking him.

Her eyes alight on him. The sketch of a smile spreads across her lips.

He stands up. Smiles back at her.

His heart skips a beat or two or three.

She stands there motionless, as the arriving crowds mill all around her, a statue of perfection at the centre of the hurly-burly of the airport.

She slips her rucksack from her shoulders. He moves toward her, feeling all around him freeze, like a slow motion scene in a movie with the soft rock soundtrack missing and replaced by a cacophony of disruptive languages in a cocktail of voices.

Inches apart.

The heat from her body reaches toward him, a hint of spearmint on her breath.

'Hello, Louise.'

'Hi there.'

She leans over, kisses him on the right cheek.

He briefly imagines she's telling herself he's so much older than she thought, fatter, less than handsome.

'For a moment, I thought you weren't coming,' he says, as behind her the luggage begins to accumulate on the conveyor belt.

'I said I would come,' she answers. 'Why should I not?'

'I'm just rather insecure,' he says.

'I'm a lot of things,' she smiles. 'But not that.'

'So, no regrets?' he asks her.

'Not yet,' she tells him. 'You asked me to come. Here I am.'

'Good,' is all he can summon as an answer. Then, 'What does your case look like? We'll look out for it.'

'I haven't one,' she says, pointing at the rucksack at her feet. 'This is all I've brought. Some change of underwear. For my first time in New York I thought it would be nice to buy some new clothes while I'm here.'

He smiles. 'We can buy them together. That would be nice.'

'Sure.'

'They must have been surprised when you checked in back in London, no? Travelling so light?'

'I just said I was a student.'

'I see,' he says.

She bends to retrieve her rucksack.

'Shall we?' she asks.

'Yes.' He picks up his case. 'Let's go and find a cab.'

The driver must be from Haiti, he reckons. His radio is tuned to a station full of static, reggae and rap and French patois.

She sits close to him on the back seat. He tries to recognise the perfume she is wearing.

JFK Boulevard. Van Wyck Expressway. Jamaica. Queens. Past La Guardia and the mortal remains of some long past exhibition by a dirty lake. The car is held up for fifteen minutes on the approach to the Midtown Tunnel. The driver puts a hand through the partition, requesting toll money. He still has a pocketful of coins from his last trip to America. He'd been promoting his latest book, a study of contemporary French literature. The joys of a five-city East Coast tour.

In the darkness of the tunnel, she places her hand on his. Since meeting up at the airport, they have barely spoken. Mostly about the weather; here, back in London, in the south of France where he now lives. How their respective flights had gone. Had she managed to sleep, and how he had spent the time reading. The in-flight movies and meals. Small talk at its most banal.

They finally drive out of the tunnel into the canyons of Manhattan and he breathes a sigh of relief. In the hotel room, he knows, he will be more eloquent, less shy and tongue-tied.

The traffic in the cross streets slows them down further as they navigate the traffic lights up to midtown.

They finally reach the hotel he has booked them into. Not the usual one where most staff in reception know him already, but one close by. He pays the cab driver. A porter rushes forward to assist with the luggage. There is only his case propped in the cab boot against a worn spare tyre. She carries her rucksack by its strap, and straightens her blue skirt as she steps out of the yellow vehicle.

He catches the porter's glance. Feels suddenly like a guilty, dirty old man, with this young girl at his side. Twenty-five years age difference. I am a cliché, he thinks. Damn it, he's not going to feel guilt now, is he?

At reception they make a big fuss of him. Ten years since he has stayed here last, according to the computer.

The elevator. The long corridor festooned with Andy Warhol prints. He inserts the electronic card key into the slot, the door flashes green and opens.

'Welcome to New York, Louise,' he says as a wave of infinite tenderness washes over his heart.

There is little for him to unpack as she uses the bathroom to freshen up from the journey. He listens to the water splash behind the door as he hangs his shirts and jackets in the cupboard. It's only mid-afternoon.

She emerges. Smiling sweetly. Now she looks even younger. Wonderfully slim, her loose dark hair falling over her shoulders, reaching midway down her back. Her waist looks as if he could hold it within his two outstretched hands. Her breasts jut against the thin material of her white cotton T-shirt, and his eyes can't avert themselves from the hypnotic shapes that strain the alignment of the whiteness. He guesses the strap of a bra over her shoulders but the cups must be soft and barely disguise the ever-aroused state of their contents.

'Are you hungry?' he asks her.

'Not really,' she answers. 'I snacked on the plane. But it wasn't very nice, I must say.'

'It never is,' he remarks. 'Because of the time difference with Europe, I always find it better to have a meal when I get here, as late as possible. Puts one's body clock on New York time. Otherwise, we'll end up waking in the middle of the night and we'll feel even more tired.'

'If you want,' Louise says. 'Is it what they call jet-lag?'

He nods. Gazes at her.

Her eyes are pale brown, a delicate colour variation he would give heaven and hell to be able to define. The knot in his stomach grows ever more painful with every passing minute. Eventually, he knows, he will have to get to grips fully with this crazy situation he has somehow engineered.

'Shall we go out? Maybe down to the Village. Have a walk. I'll show you around. Maybe see some shops for you. Have a bite to eat.'

'Whatever.'

It's spring. The sun is out. Everything feels unreal.

They walk. It feels like miles, but neither of them are tired. They browse. He can't help visiting a few bookstores. She gets a top at Urban Outfitters, but will not let him pay. He introduces her to a Belgian chocolate bar that's not available in Europe. They have an early dinner, around seven, in a Thai restaurant on Third Avenue, near the corner of St Mark's Place. Night falls. They are about to catch a cab back to their hotel when a pea-coloured chenille sweater catches her attention in the dimly-lit window of a thrift store. This time, he insists on paying. As they exit the shop, she pulls her purchase out of its paper bag and slips it on.

'It's suddenly grown colder, hasn't it?' she remarks.

'Yes,' he agrees.

There is sea of yellow cabs cruising down the Avenue, all with their lights on. He extends his arm to hail one. The driver is from the Ukraine, and insists on practising his English on them when he discovers that he hails from England. He has relatives in Swindon, and is surprised to learn he has never actually come across them. He answers that he now lives in France. Louise remains silent about her London origins.

There is a new porter on duty at the hotel door. To avoid judgment on their apparent age difference or the risk of being told he cannot bring young ladies into the hotel – a thought that has dominated his mind throughout the cab ride up from the East Village – he exaggeratedly holds his card key aloft as they walk into the hotel. Possibly guessing his embarrassment, Louise hold his hand in hers, whether to compound his self-consciousness or reassure him, he is uncertain.

Green light.

The door opens.

The room is not overly large, the sparse furniture purports to be antique, a Picasso face is spread across the left wall, the narrow double bed – by no stretch of the imagination anywhere near king-size – dominates the landscape that is going to be theirs for the next four days. Heavy brocade curtains are drawn. It's a quiet room; he is not sure whether the window gives on to Fifth Avenue or not.

She drops her rucksack to the floor, kicks off her flat shoes and approaches the bed. Tests its firmness with her hand and then sits on its edge as he watches her. She pulls the new sweater over her head. Looks him in the eyes.

He remains silent.

Attempting to put off the inevitable, maybe?

'So?' he finally ventures, 'am I what you expected?'

The wrong age, the wrong middle-age spread, the wrong short-sighted eyes, the wrong kind of clothes, the wrong size cock, the wrong man?

'I don't know,' she replies. 'You tell me.'

Then, as an afterthought, 'but I do like your voice.'

'Is it the voice of a Master, or the voice of a slave?' he asks her.

'Do you really want me to answer that question now?' Louise says.

'You're right. I don't. Maybe you can tell me at the end of the week.'

'Exactly. I've agreed to come here with you, but I can only

be myself, you know that already...'

'Yes,' he quickly interrupts her. 'And as we talked before, back then, I respect your nature, I shall not attempt to change it. You are what you are, I accept that fully.'

'Good. I'm not seeking to be rescued...'

'I understand...'

'I am yours for this week we shall spend together in this room. Totally. Do to me what you will. Use me. Beat me. Humiliate me. My only pleasure is in giving myself. For you, I will be no different than I have been for others, with others. My holes are yours. All I am is a body, with holes made to be filled, used...'

Hearing her say it like this hurt even more than when she had initially written it.

But he tried to show no sign of the torment spiralling across his heart.

'I understand,' he repeated.

As she rises to her feet, she utters the last words he will hear from her until the following morning, 'I know there will be tenderness, but please, oh please, do not fall in love with me.' Thereafter, there were sounds. In abundance. But no more words. Only moans, sighs, cries, the whole orchestral palette of sex.

She approaches him. Closer than they have ever been.

Her lips move toward his.

They kiss.

She tastes of Middle-Eastern tea.

He takes her into his arms. Holds her tight as their kiss continues. Tongue. Teeth. Breath held back. His hands now linger all over her, feeling her softness, exploring her warmth, he feels her eager responsiveness as tremors of lust race through his body. He takes a step back, interrupting their feverish embrace. Recalls all she has revealed of her subservient nature.

'Undress,' he orders her.

Her eyes look up towards the light fixture.

'One item at a time,' he continues. 'I want to examine your body.'

She lowers her eyes and proceeds to pull the white T-shirt off, twisting its folds over her head, mussing her long brown hair which falls back down on her shoulders. Her skin is porcelain white. His heart tightens as sudden memories of another woman with the same pale skin flood back through his mind. Small flowery patterns crisscross the flimsy flesh-coloured bra she is wearing. It has no under-wiring. Her small, pert breasts clearly don't require any. Her hands move to her back and she unhooks the bra and her chest is fully revealed. There is a dark mole an inch or so below her left nipple. Discreet dots of pigmentation are scattered across the approach to her modest cleavage, too pale even to merit the epithet of freckles.

The golden rings hang from her nipples, catching a fleeting reflection of the light from the hotel room's ceiling fixture and its three low-wattage bulbs. They are thin, half the diameter of a wedding ring. She watches his eyes alight on them. She straightens her back, offering her ringed breasts to him. He extends a hand, touches the metal adornments. They feel light. Carefully he twists one of the rings and observes the way the darker, puckered flesh of her nipple follows the movement of the ring between his fingers. Her gaze is unflinching. He twists further, and with a finger of his other hand begins to manipulate the other ring in similar fashion. He watches as the pierced nipples harden and lengthen imper-ceptibly as he continues to manipulate the gold rings and her nipples. He pulls on one of them and he sees her flinch. But she says nothing.

Finally, he lets go and allows his now-free hands to roam over her shoulders, caress her back. His plunges his fingers into her loose hair, pulls her head back and kisses her again, his tongue delving as deep as he can manage toward her throat. He can feel the rhythmic beat of her heart.

Her sharp nails begin to scratch his own back.

He keeps his eyes open as he kisses her. Notices the faint pale pink scar on her upper lip. Almost shaped like the letter N. Remembers its origin: Nola and the male friend also called N were drunk and had heated a paper clip in the flame of a lighter until it glowed red and tried to brand her with their joint initial.

He pushes Louise gently away.

'Suck me,' he tells her.

Nude to the waist down, like a fragile doll in her blue, now billowing skirt, she lowers herself to her knees, face in alignment with his crotch, and unclips his belt, unbuttons the top of his trousers and pulls them down to his knees. He is already partly hard and his cock is straining against his dark grey boxer shorts, an obscene bump of maleness.

She inserts a finger under the elastic and releases the cock.

He realises momentarily that he probably smells down there: the eight hours flight and sweat, the long afternoon walk, the sweat, the heat. He should have washed first.

Her mouth approaches. Her tongue licks his shaft, slowly, tantalisingly; a hand cups his heavy, dark balls and her lips close in on the glans as she takes him into her mouth. The heat is wonderful. She allows him all the way in, his tip bumping against the back of her throat. She doesn't gag as she impales her mouth over him. No woman has taken him in so far without choking. She has, he knows, been mercilessly trained by previous users under dire threat of punishment or violence. His cock grows inside her mouth.

Her tongue surrounds his hardness, dancing lightly around his captured stem, teasing, licking, caressing. Her lips hold him in a soft but firm vice, slip sliding over his engorged flesh, welcoming his invasion, wordlessly inviting him to thrust ever deeper into her.

His eyes wander across the horizon of the room. The Picasso head is watching them as the young girl studiously keeps on sucking his middle-aged cock.

At this rate, he knows, he won't last much longer. He does not wish to come so soon, inside her mouth. He retreats, withdraws from her mouth. She looks up at him, puzzled, thinking maybe she hasn't performed well enough and is due for punishment.

He attempts a smile of kindness to reassure her.

'Undress,' he asks her. 'Take the rest off now.'

She obeys.

Stands up and unzips the blue skirt. It slips to the hotel room carpet. The shape of her body is the nearest he has come to witnessing perfection, outside of doubtlessly doctored photographs in magazines. At the age of twenty neither gravity nor the ravages of time have yet taken hold and begun their seditious work.

Her knickers are modest, thick white cotton, practical, sexless.

She bends over slightly to pull them down.

He knows what to expect. From what she has written.

He also knows it's the first thing that initially attracted him to her, and convinced him he had to see her one day. A prurient curiosity that betrays the filth in him.

The bunched-up piece of white underwear now lies in a small heap on the carpet. She straightens up. His eyes move up her smooth legs. Slowly. Almost hesitantly.

It's as he knew it would be.

His turn to move to his knees and bring his face to her genital area.

Quite hairless, both above and around her cunt. Like the crotch of a doll or a pre-pubescent girl.

Not a wisp of hair, not even a darker shadow of hairs past. The same milky white shade that characterises her whole body.

And the rings.

Gold.

Each one a thin band, like a cheap wedding ring.

Eight of them.

Four hanging from each labia, in perfect alignment, pulling both outer lips out of the central gash, the darker, redder skin like meaty folds on a butcher's stall, raw, almost bloody, as if the necessary piercings had only been done recently.

He gasps.

Incongruously wonders whether there is enough metal here to set off airport alarms.

Each set of labial rings are held together by a thin contraption of stainless steel, like a nurse's large safety pin with three branches. The middle one is threaded through all the rings while the two outer ones squeeze the pin tight and the whole is kept closed by a minuscule padlock.

He advances his fingers, gingerly touches the chastity device protecting her entrance, and his hand feels the intense heat emanating from the invisible depths of her cunt.

The rings effectively seal her tight. There is not even space to insert a finger. As she had warned him. Even at period time, she is unable to use a tampon and has to rely on sanitary towels.

'It's awesome,' he whispers in the now hushed silence of the room. 'It's... beautiful.' And barbaric, he thinks, but he is so turned on.

He can't take his eyes off her locked cunt.

She remains quite silent.

Observing him.

Judging him?

This older man, with his thinning hair, his cock jutting out as if on military parade, his love handles, the sombre bags under his eyes, his trousers bunched up around his ankles.

He finally takes off the rest of his clothes and asks Louise to lay down on the bed, on her back, and indicates she should open her legs wide.

He kneels, forces the angle between her thighs even wider and examines her like a doctor, mentally storing every detail of her adornments, her mutilation, as he gazes at the brazen display of the wonder of her jewelled portals.

He moves his face against her cunt, feels her inner warmth vibrate toward his cheeks, tries to slip his tongue between the minute gaps between the rings, but there is no access. She is utterly sealed.

Louise extends a hand, musses his air, sensing his obvious frustration.

He is on his knees at the foot of the bed, his head at the apex of her thighs, inhaling deeply, trying to seize the ineffable smell of her.

The sheer hardness of his cock weighs against his stomach.

He thinks of investing her mouth again, but Louise shifts on her side and repositions herself on all fours on the bed, her rump raised toward him. A perfect, pale sphere, punctured by the darker heart of her anus; both her hands move back to either side and stretch her globes apart, inviting him. He wets his cock and thrusts himself into her arse in one swift movement. His head punctures the tight sphincter and his whole cock is quickly embedded inside her. She shifts to accommodate him better.

He digs inside her and for the next ten minutes, an eternity, he fucks her arse watching the skin around her aperture distend with every in and out movement of his thick cock. He moans. She moans. He sweats. The perspiration drops from his forehead to his chin and then onto her back, where it pools slowly, a small transparent pond of humidity vibrating intensely to the accompaniment of every tremor that crosses her body as he tries to force himself ever deeper into her bowels. His lips are dry. She bites hers, out of pleasure or pain. His heart beats a light fantastic. Picasso is on the wall. They are bathed in the clandestine sounds of the hotel. Their fuck is an island of motion cut off from the rest of the world. He holds back as long as he can manage. Below the dark piston of his cock and its mechanical assault of her innards, the rings shine, wetness from above and inside her bathing them in an unmistakable sheen of lust. His frenzied eyes mirror his soul, flitting from arsehole to ring-bedecked cunt, and his hardness just refuses to fade away.

Her sounds of sex are silent. Gentle cries, repressed gasps, deep breaths. She adjusts the position of her body to accommodate his movements, to accept him even deeper, her sphincter muscles tightening rhythmically around him before releasing his penis again, then tightening again capturing every renewed attack. His tip is deep inside her bowels. Where it burns. And feels good.

Finally, he can hold out no longer. Louise's whole body is just made for sex, a finely-honed machine for the benefit of his pleasure. He comes. He roars. Her name. A profanity. Feels his come burst out of him and bathing her insides, like a river of sin, a torrent out of control. He rests his hands on the bed, bent over her, the beat of his breath returning to normality. Silence. At last, he feels his hardness begin to recede and pulls back, withdrawing his still pulsating cock from her. It emerges, bathed in come and inner juices. Her hole is shockingly dilated, red raw at the edges, like a small dark bottomless crevice. Never has he witnessed a sight so pornographic and, at the same time, so shockingly beautiful. The temporary scar his raging cock has left on her.

But he also knows she did not come.

They lie down together, moist body against pale body.

'Tired?' he asks her.

He pulls the covers over their bare bodies.

She nods, her eyes half-closed.

'It's the jet-lag catching up,' he says. It's only ten at night in Manhattan.

He wakes at two in the morning, still 9pm European time, with a hard on, his mind and body in tumult. She is on her side, her back to him. He pulls her sleeping body toward him and the contact of her flesh only accentuates his desire. He pushes a finger into her arsehole. She is still dripping, leaking his earlier come. He slips his cock into her and begins fucking her again. It takes him ages to orgasm as he rages against her with every movement, angrily seeking release. At one stage, he surprises himself and finds his hands beginning to tighten around her thin neck as his thrusts take a vengeful rhythm. He quickly releases the pressure of his fingers there. He doesn't know whether she is awake or still sleeping. But her whole body accepts him.

He awakes again; there is a thin sliver of light peering through the heavy curtains. Early morning. This time Louise is no longer sleeping, busy sucking on his cock with greedy appetite. Her eyes stay closed, he sees, as she does this.

When he is fully erect, she squats above him, stretches her rump cheeks open and plants herself on his cock, once again taking him deep into her arse. When he finally comes, the feeling is so strong, he thinks he is going to pass out.

'So, do I please you?' she asks, her first words since the previous evening.

'Yes, Louise, you do,' he answers.

Q & A

'So who is Nola?'

'She's my half-sister.'

'How old were you?'

'Sixteen.'

'Tell me about it, her and you. How it happened.'

'I was born in a well-off, heavily Catholic family. We weren't rich, but life was easy and I was spoilt as a child. My sister is somewhat older than me. I've always believed she was very unhappy about my arrival at such a late stage. The family had been in flux with remarriages on both sides. But there was money.'

'How did she become aware of your submissive tendencies?'

'I think that she somehow always knew.'

'And she exploited it? You must hate her.'

'No, I don't. I love her, feel very close to her.'

'When did she first take advantage of this knowledge?'

'I was a good pupil at school, but I excelled in sports. I particularly enjoyed gymnastics, I was told I had talent. For my sixteenth birthday, I asked for private lessons in one of the City's better clubs. My parents agreed to it, and I was signed in for lessons two evenings a week and following school on Wednesday afternoons. Nola insisted on accompanying me, as a chaperone of sorts. I remember her often mocking me when I was younger, because of my lack of feminine opulence. 'The Plank' when I was thirteen, later 'No Bum' when I reached fourteen. My body developed late.'

'Your half-sister seduced you?'

'Not quite. She was very pleasant to me during the course of the early lessons. She watched my training and soon recognised my innate talent and the suppleness of my body. Initially, I attended the lessons wearing shorts and a T-shirt, but soon the teacher asked me to wear a dancer's leotard so that she might able to supervise and see how all my muscles worked. She taught me a lot, often correcting my stance or the use of the wrong muscles with a small wooden cane. Nola befriended her and was soon assigned to holding the cane.'

'She beat you?'

'Lesson after lesson, the instructions became more and more difficult to follow and she would strike me harder, with the assent of the instructor. I always felt they were in total collusion. Surprisingly, I began to look forward to her striking me, even though it was sometimes painful. To this day, I still hanker to submit to her; she was so beautiful. So tall and her hair so dark and red. And her severity struck an unusually responsive chord inside me as I took instruction. I think I had basically been submissive in spirit ever since my early childhood.'

'How come?'

'Even as a child, I recall never wishing to be a princess when we played games with my sisters or friends. I preferred to imagine myself as a servant.'

'How did the relationship progress to you becoming, so to speak, her slave?'

'After the course of lessons came to an end. I continued my gymnastics training, this time solely under Nola's supervision. Soon, she began to realise, I think, that I was sometimes making deliberate mistakes, and she began striking me for no reason at all, and noted that I did not object. One day, for the first time, she struck me badly with her long, thin cane before our session even began. Told me it was to encourage me. She had guessed my masochist nature. That day, following our work-out, I deliberately followed her into the shower and confessed how attractive I found her and that I was in love with her. She surprised me by replying that she had lusted after me ever since I had been younger, and her earlier taunts had just been indications of her disguised desire for me. We kissed.'

'And?'

'She warned me of her dominant character and that, in

any form of relationship, I would have to submit to her will. I readily agreed. She made love to me there and then under the shower. It was heavenly. She knew every spot to touch, as if by magic.'

'Had you been with boys before?'

'Somehow, I had never been attracted to men much. I'd kissed one or two boys, even allowed one to fondle my breasts under my shirt, but I hadn't ventured further.'

'You were still only sixteen?'

'Yes. From the next day onward, I began following Nola's instructions. I wanted only to please her. She said I should no longer wear jeans and dress like a tomboy. I must always wear dresses or skirts, no pantyhose, only stockings. Every day after school, I would go to her room and wait for her to return from her own lessons or the bookshop where she sometimes worked on a part-time basis. She would often leave instructions for me on small pieces of paper on the kitchen table. This was a time when our parents were often away travelling and we had to fend for ourselves. I had to follow these most precisely. One day, she left an apron for me to wear, alongside the note. I was to become her servant.'

'What was the sex like?'

'In bed, she was brutal and authoritarian. She enjoyed ordering me around, loved to humiliate me, sometimes inflicted much pain. But I enjoyed it more than I had enjoyed anything in my life before.'

'I don't want to sound like a dime store psychiatrist, but had you previously felt unloved, unwanted at home?'

'Not at all. It's just the way I am. I don't think anything will ever change my nature.'

'How did things develop, then with Nola?'

'After three months of living like this, rushing to her room every day straight from school, all feverish, anxious for more of her harsh love and punishment, desperately trying to get away from college work over the week-ends to spend more time with her, I just decided to leave school altogether and put myself completely at Nola's service.'

'Did your parents suspects anything?'

'This was the time when they moved to Belgium. Nola said she was old enough to look after me. After all, we'd been on our own for long periods of time already. We weren't kids any longer. So we were both given a generous allowance.'

'So, you lived alone with Nola from then on?'

'I was her maid during the day and her toy at night. She became even harder on me now, would not accept a word of disobedience, insisted on only the highest standards of house work, cleaning and cooking. Whenever I failed, or forgot an instruction, the beating was most severe. The worse it became, the happier I was.'

'Tell me how.'

'For Valentine's Day, she bought a whip and a pair of handcuffs for me. The whip was to be used on me, of course. Thereafter, most days she handcuffed me before leaving for her work. Thus constricted, she said I would have more time to think of her all day. Naturally, my work around the house suffered badly. Which gave her even more opportunities to use the whip on me. But sex with her after every whipping was better than ever. I could wish for no other fate. Very soon, she began to use the whip on my body for no other reason than arousing me further sexually. Now she no longer even needed a reason to beat me, mark me.'

'And you enjoyed this?'

'I was deliriously happy. This was what I was born to be. Later, she would take me to the West End and Soho on special shopping trips to a basement store that specialised in fetish and S&M apparel. She bought increasingly sophisticated devices and clothing for me. She would make me wear elaborate black leather outfits that made me look like a whore at a sadomasochists' convention. She had me play with toys in front of the assistants in the store as she exercised her power. Would have me gagged, plugged, displayed. Force me to wear underwear she had deliberately dirtied before. Back at her home, I had to serve her completely, in every detail. It soon became my task to lick her clean after she had been to the toilet. She loved me and I loved her. I thought this bliss would last forever.'

Mid-morning in the Manhattan hotel room. He calls out for bagels from Mom's Bagel's two streets away. For him, a garlic bialy with Nova Scotia lox and cream cheese, and a plain bagel with cream cheese and jelly for her.

They devour the food in bed, close to each other. He feels comfortable with her, their bare bodies touch as they shift, neither draws back from the contact. He loves the fact that, like him, she is a creature of silence, doesn't find it necessary to make small talk and fill every precious moment of silence with needless words. A thin dollop of red jelly drops on to her left breast. He bends over and licks her clean, his furtive tongue nibbling on her ring, stretching the tender skin beneath. A warm feeling suffuses his abdomen. Blood already coursing back towards his tired cock.

Aware he is probably in no condition to perform again yet, he draws back and takes the kiss to her lips.

She smiles.

They have opened the curtains. Sunlight floods the room, the bed, their uncovered bodies.

He tells her about the last time he stayed here. For two nights in a row a couple in the room next door had practised particularly noisy sex, the sounds of which could just not be avoided through the thin wall, keeping him awake and arousing his own lust. The woman had been especially vocal, every thrust inside her provoking further moans, gasps or profane vocabulary in her lexicon of pleasure. The man, on the other hand, appeared to copulate in silence, leaving all vocal accompaniment up to his partner, but must have had incredible staying power as the sounds of their frantic lovemaking reverberated through to his room for almost two hours. On and on the sounds of nearby sex continued and he had begun to wonder what this shrill, enthusiastic woman might actually look like. The following night, the carnival occurred again in the adjoining room. On the third day, as he was leaving his room for his morning appointments, he finally caught a glimpse of a woman closing the door to the next room. To his disappointment and amazement – by now, he had visions in his mind of Greek goddesses or hardcore stars of the pornographic screen – she was a stocky, matronly Chinese woman in an old-fashioned fur coat draped across her shoulders, wearing sensible shoes and with a chignon in her hair. Anything but his dreams.

Louise laughs at his story.

'Well, I don't think we bothered the neighbours much,' she remarks. 'We're both wordless fornicators, I noticed.'

He smiles back at her. Preferring not to tell her his other story of a hotel room fuck. In Paris, window opening on to a sea of Latin Quarter roofs. Where the sounds of the adjoining room had in fact been more muted but still caught his attention. Aroused, he had taken a glass from the bathroom and stuck it against the separating wall, cupped his ear against it and listened to the couple frolicking a few inches away, and masturbated to the sound of their fucking.

Finally, they get up.

In the light of day, he finds her more beautiful than ever. And younger. Less than half his age.

'Who gets to use the bathroom first?' he asks her.

'You go,' she answers. 'I feel wonderfully lazy this morning.'

He shaves. Christ, does he look tired! The new razor blade
revives his skin. He washes the foam away and cleans his
teeth. He tests the heat of the water bursting from out of the
shower head, finds the right balance of hot and cold and steps
into the shower. He is soaping his cock, washing away their
combined juices, when he hears her knock on the bathroom
door.

'Yes?'

'Can I come in?' she asks him.

'Of course,' he replies. There is no need for false modesty
now.

She tiptoes in, walks across the damp tiles and sits herself
on the toilet bowl. Facing him, legs wide apart, she proceeds
to pee as he stands under the pouring water just a few feet
away. He notices the eight rings hanging loosely from her
labia as the thick stream of urine jets out of her, and realises
the safety pin and the padlock are no longer in place. His first
glance at the pinkness inside her cunt as her leaves separate,
gape, to make way for the release of her warm stream.

She looks up at him, with a wry smile on her lips.

His eyes interrogate her silently.

'You never asked,' she says, as the last drops of pee keep
on dribbling out of her. 'A real Master always does, he
orders.'

'I didn't realise…' he mumbles.

'I was allowed to bring the padlock key with me,' she con-
firms.

'I see,' is all he can feebly say. Feeling as if he has failed the
first test.

'Can I join you under the shower?' Louise asks.

'Of course,' he says.

Her body shines under the pounding water. They embrace.
Kiss. Separate. Their hair soaking wet now. United by the
cleansing spurts of hot water. They soap each other with all

the delicacy they can muster. Kiss again. They step out of the shower. He turns to switch the water off and when he turns again to face her, she delicately takes his cock in her wet fingers.

'There was still some soap,' she says.

She squeezes it. Hard.

He takes her hand away.

'Stay like that,' he says.

She remains immobile, water still dripping down the expanse of her body. He takes hold of a towel and dries her, enveloping her body in its softness. He glides his finger through her hair.

'Oh, Louise,' he says.

'Yes?' she asks.

'I want to make love to you properly now,' he answers.

He bends and picks her up in his arms. She is so light, he notices; and they make their way from steamy bathroom to the bed in the hotel room now blinded with light.

He pulls a curtain half-closed. There is still enough light for him to see all of her.

He installs her on the bed. She remains inert. Her opening gapes, as if alive, breathing like an invitation to pleasure. He delicately spreadeagles her limbs in a semblance of crucifixion across the crumpled sheets and buries his face in her cunt. He opens her up at long last and spies the infinite nacreous shades of her inner walls. Parting her, rings to each side, he plunges his tongue inside her and a tremor flashes through her whole body. She still tastes of soap but her juices are soon abundantly flowing, pungent, aromatic, overflowing, bathing his chin as he labours away now, playing with her engorged clit. He has reached his destination, her portals of paradise. The velvet pearl pulses strongly against the tip of his tongue. Louise moans. Widens the angle of her legs further in acceptance of his adoration. His face retreats. He looks up at her.

Her face and the whole area leading to her breasts are flushed a deep hue of pink. Her eyes are closed.

He inserts a finger, then two, inside her cunt. She is like a furnace inside. He moves his other free hand towards her rear and sticks a finger inside her arsehole, where she is still gooey from their earlier exertions. Louise gasps as both her holes are invaded.

Through the incandescent body heat, he feels the pulse of her heart beat against his probing fingers. He bends, withdraws the digits and takes her now protuberant clit between his teeth and nibbles away at it. He feels her close to coming, for the first time since they have been together. His mouth takes leave of her copiously flowing juices and he climbs over her and inserts his cock inside her.

A wordless sound passes her lips.

Tenderness sweeps across his heart as he begins moving inside her. The fit is exquisite. The gold rings on either side of her cunt lips slide effortlessly against his shaft, enhancing the sensations without overpowering them. As he thrusts in and out of her, the thought occurs to him that if he were her Master he would have her pierced yet again, a ring or a stud in her clitoris, just to enhance the friction against his glans as it labours and retreats against her opening time and again. Yes, a nice thought. And a big if.

He closes his eyes in turn and surrenders to their first moment of love.

Q & A

'How did things begin to change in your relationship?'

'She liked to show me off to others. Demonstrate the extent of her power over me.'

'Men? Women?'

'She would invite friends to our house and play at humiliating me in front of them.'

'How?'

'By having me wear the outfits she had bought for me. Playing games she knew I was bound to lose and then punishing me for my mistakes. I would have to strip in front of her guests and have my rear caned or whipped. If there were other women, she would make me lick her sex in their presence, sometimes had me lie on the floor while they peed over me. I would have to serve food naked but for a dog collar and was forbidden to react while they pinched me, touched my intimate parts, sometimes tried to trip me to cause further punishment.'

'But were there men?'

'Initially, only one. A close friend of hers. His name was N. He's a lawyer from the city.'

'Was he her lover?'

'No, Nola hates men, sexually. But she was close to N. She liked exposing me to him, making me bend over so that he could peer inside me, even touch, which she knew I hated. The more ill at ease I was in these situations, the more it excited her and the crueller she became with him as witness to my degradation.'

'What sort of things would she do for him?'

'She liked to demonstrate my absolute obedience. One day, I was made to lie on my back on the floor as she inserted a series of ever-larger objects inside my vagina which I had to hold wide open for them. First a dildo, then a bottle, then a cucumber. All the time, I could see the bump inside his trousers swell as she teased him and said wouldn't he like it to be him in that nice virgin cunt.'

'You were still a virgin?'

'Technically, yes. I hadn't yet been penetrated by a man. By Nola and objects only.'

'How did it happen, the first time?'

'With N. One morning, Nola summoned me and

instructed me that I should take a taxi to his apartment and do every single thing he would ask me to do. When I protested, she whipped me badly. Said I did not understand what true love was. I argued that I did. But she owed N some debt, and he wanted me and that was that. Anyway, she told me, it would be good for my training, I had to be broken in. I went to him. Hated every moment. Later, there were other men she loaned me to.'

'Did she ever want to watch you being fucked by them?'

'No. If she was there, she would move to another room.'

'But did she ever ask you about what happened with the men?'

'Curiously, no. Although I was avid to tell her all, to demonstrate the extent of my affection for her by describing the pain they had inflicted on me, how they had used me, violated all my holes, made me choke on their filthy penises and forced me to swallow their ejaculate, played with me, beat me too. I wanted to tell her, Nola, I have accepted all this for your sake. But she never asked. And if there were marks, cuts, bruises on my body, she would whip me in response, as if it were all my fault.'

'Sounds very much like one-way traffic to me.'

'She said that the coming of my seventeenth birthday would mark a significant point in our relationship. That I had satisfied her so far and she would show me her gratitude on this occasion.'

'What did she do?'

'We drove to Hastings on a Saturday morning. I thought she would be getting me new outfits at the Soho fetish shop, but this was not the case. It was a large building in the suburbs of the resort, a doctor she knew well. I would come across him again at the special parties. He used electrolysis to depilate my pubic area. I'm told it will never grow back again. Then, he pierced my breasts and fitted the rings I still have now. I was in heaven. I was Nola's slave, in both body and spirit.'

'What are those special parties you mentioned?'

'They occurred later. I will tell you.'

'OK.'

Their second full day in Manhattan. The spring weather is clement. They walk. Catch cabs. Shop. Snack. Battery Park. The Cloisters. Central Park, watching the squirrels hop along the scarce vegetation.

They talk.

'Are you happy?' he asks her. 'It's such fun showing you this city, all these places I have known and liked for years. I try and imagine what it feels for you to see them for the first time.'

'It's nice,' she answers. 'But you're too soft with me. I don't deserve this, you know. If I were in your place, I would be crueller, much harder. Somehow I think you're too sensitive. Almost like a girl...'

His face clouds over.

'If you were in charge and I was a girl, would you fuck me?' he quietly inquires.

'I would,' Louise says. 'I would stretch you, hurt you until you plead for mercy, but I wouldn't give you any. I have been taught well. Switching is no problem.'

'I see.'

'Would you prove your devotion to me by letting me treat you like that?' Louise asks him as they cross toward the Plaza Hotel.

He doesn't hesitate.

'I would,' he replies.

'OK,' she says.

They catch a cab which takes them to a dark side street near the Port Authority Terminal. In a sex shop manned by Pakistani assistants they buy a strap-on dildo. Flesh coloured, veined, awesomely realistic and life-size. And handcuffs. So that he doesn't change his mind, she says.

He is in no hurry to return to their hotel room.

He reminds her she wanted to go to Macy's.

She wanders indifferently through the designer label departments.

'I want to buy you something nice,' he insists.

'Why?' she queries. 'How do you want me to dress? Like a whore or a princess?'

'As a young woman.'

She agrees to stockings, a silk cream-coloured see-through blouse and a flowing skirt in rainbow colours.

They arrive back at the hotel mid-afternoon. The room has been made, and the smells of sex have faded.

'Undress,' she orders him, herself stripping from the waist downwards and fitting the strap-on around her waist. He notices she has reattached the safety pin and the padlock.

He silently sheds his clothes, takes a step towards the bathroom, planning to wash the sweat away from his body.

'Don't,' she forbids him. 'I want you dirty, I want to smell your vileness as I fuck you.'

He knows he shouldn't protest; his face reddens as his arse crack feels all clammy, and his feet sticky.

'On your knees. NOW!'

He gets down on all fours.

'Raise your head.'

He does. His eyes are parallel with her labial rings, he notices she is seeping there. She is excited. She thrusts the artificial cock toward his mouth.

'Suck me,' she intimates.

The rubbery material fills his mouth, the taste is unpleasant. She only lets him suck the dildo for a minute or two then withdraws it and places herself behind him. All she wanted was for him to wet it.

She places the strap-on head against his anus and begins pushing it in.

It enters him with surprising ease. Initially, there is little pain and he is almost disappointed.

The feeling doesn't last and soon he is biting his lips to repress heartfelt sounds of anguish as Louise goes to war on him. Viciously twisting the implement of torture within his gut as she endlessly adjusts her stance to increase its depth, the angle of attack and the unremitting pressure on his protesting bowels. He knows she is enjoying this. But he reasons, beyond the valley of pain, that she deserves at least this; that this is his own particular way of experiencing some of the humiliation that has been lavished on her by so many others. He communes with her as she keeps on fucking his arse, until the skin inside and outside of the hole is raw and mutilated from the friction. His heart beats wildly, bile pools at the back of his throat, he has difficulty breathing. There is no longer any pleasure in the act for him.

Then, as suddenly as she entered him, she pulls it out in one swift movement and he momentarily feels as his whole insides are being suctioned out.

He collapses, stomach first, onto the floor.

'There,' she says. 'I think you would make a better slave than Master. Very docile. You take your suffering in silence; that's a a good sign,' she remarks.

For a moment, the germ of an idea settles in his mind. An image of the two of them as slaves, collared together, made to perform for the benefit of others.

At last, he rises, as his breath returns. Louise now sits on the bed, watching him. The strap now detached from her, her hands shielding her jewelled pubes.

'I hurt you, didn't I?' she asks, watching him rub his hole with the back of his hand. There is some blood.

'You did,' he says.

'Then I must be punished,' she says. 'That is the way.'

As he washes the traces of the fuck away some minutes later, he realises she is now testing him. It's scary: could he ever become her Master? Keep her?

He dresses.

The crease of his boxer shorts rubs painfully against his bruised flesh as he walks back into the room. Louise is watching a game show on the TV set.

'I'm taking you out,' he tells her, switching the programme off.

'Where to?'

'Never you mind.'

Somehow he always knew it would come to this.

She understands.

Asks: 'How should I dress?'

'Like a whore. Wear that blouse and no bra, and stockings. And your shortest skirt. No underwear.'

She nods.

Night falls as their cab rushes down Fifth toward SoHo. He instructs her. At all times, she will sit with her legs open; there is to be no false modesty. She is his property for tonight and the following day and he will broach no disobedience. She will only talk when spoken to. She indicates her assent to his terms.

'You will take no pleasure from what is done to you, because I won't either...'

'A Master would take pleasure in displaying me,' she interrupts him.

He slaps her cheek, as punishment for her uncalled verbal response.

'Quiet, now.'

Her cheek reddens from the blow. She lowers her eyes. The driver looks inquiringly into his rear mirror at the older man and the young woman. Even though the light outside is dimming, he clearly saw her nipples through the shimmering blouse as she entered his cab, and he tries to get a better look.

A jazz club. Grimy walls, cigarette smoke, dissonant melodies running like waves across the ceiling over the sparse audience. He has her drink vodka and orange, although he knows she dislikes the concoction. Men at the bar glance in their direction. Her skirt is hitched up to mid-thigh. He fingers her under the table. She squirms.

Her rings are wet with her secretions.

He informs her of the fact. Presents a finger to her.

'Lick me clean.'

She does, just as the waitress approaches their table inquiring after another round.

'Touching,' the waitress mumbles, visibly disapproving and mistaking Louise's appetite for a gesture of love.

'Isn't it?' he responds with a wry smile.

The tension is palpable, as he summons his courage.

She senses it and remains damningly silent and expressionless.

Finally.

'Anything?'

'Yes,' Louise replies. 'Anything, it is my nature to be a slave.'

He rises from his seat as the band on stage finish their set in a flourish of drum rolls and reverb, takes hold of her hand and they make their way to the toilets. He briefly holds his breath and then enters the men's, followed by her. There is a harsh smell of antiseptic lingering in the air, the ceiling is low, the surroundings claustrophobic. There is no one there. Just a yellowing row of urinals, a creaking fan circling like a low-flying aircraft close to the peeling, concrete ceiling, a sink with a dripping tap, a dirty towel, and behind a wooden door painted jet-black the lone toilet seat. He opens the cubicle and orders Louise to sit. He pulls her blue skirt up to her waist, unveiling her rings, and opens the buttons of her blouse so that her breasts are also on display.

'Like that. Yes.'

She doesn't answer.

'The first man to come in,' he says.

She nods silently.

They wait. Each passing second extends to eternity.

Finally the door swings open and a tall black guy walks in, hands already unzipping his flies. He heads towards the urinal, his back to Louise in the cubicle.

'Hi.'

He recognises the guy, who played bass in the band, a lanky man in denim.

'Hi, man. How ya doin'?'

'Listen. I have something for you…'

The musician starts peeing.

'Nah, man, I have my own supplier. Thanks anyway.'

'It's not drugs.'

The black guy shrugs.

'Yeah? What, then?'

'I have a woman here. She'll suck you dry for free. Interested?'

The man looks over his shoulder at him, weighing the seriousness of the offer.

Notices the open cubicle and Louise sitting there, splayed open, all her gold rings on display.

He catches his breath.

'What's in it for you?' he asks, turning round and zipping his jeans up. His eyes are now fixed on the obscene spectacle of the young woman, her white flesh like a beacon in the sordid surroundings. 'Wow,' he whispers to himself.

'I watch. That's all.'

'You serious?'

'Absolutely.'

'I'd always heard you limeys got your kicks in weird fashion,' he says, a grin spreading over his dark features.

He approaches the cubicle and its immobile prisoner. He unzips and pulls out his cock. It's long, thick, uncut. Offers it to her, hesitantly as if all this is about to disappear in a puff of smoke and is but a crazy mirage, a drug-fuelled dream. Louise bends her face forward to take the cock.

'Sweet gal,' says the musician as her lips first graze his stem, before she takes him all in. 'Will she swallow?' he asks.

'Yes,' he answers.

And watches the spectacle.

Black against white.

Black inside white.

To the bitter end.

After it is over, he allows her to adjust her apparel and cups his hands together to allow her to drink the tap water and wash her mouth.

Relief floods over him that no other man entered the bathroom while the three of them were there. He's not sure he could have controlled the situation any further.

Still, she says nothing.

They finish their drinks and listen to the first quarter of an hour of the band's second set. He hails a cab and they return to the hotel.

This is the first night in Manhattan they do not make love.

Q & A

'Did things happen that you particularly disliked?'

'Many. What I still found most difficult was when she invited friends around to demonstrate her power over me and my subservience, and took great pleasure humiliating me in their presence. The sex I didn't mind. But I did feel shame. More so, when we left the house to go to parties and she had me walk out onto the street wearing accessories and clothing which were so explicit as to provide little doubt as to my status as her personal slave. A dog collar, a skimpy maid's outfit, sometimes even a thin metal chain that connected to the handcuffs she made me wear for the short walk to the car park.'

'You were afraid that people might recognise you?'

'Not really, I did not like the fact that my slavery might be recognised by others.'

'I'm not sure I understand. You are proud of what you are.'

'I know. The worst time was when she invited a girl I thought had previously been my best friend when I was still at school along for tea to the house one evening. I hadn't seen her for nearly a year. I had to wear the maid's outfit with the apron and serve them in silence as my erstwhile friend's smile nauseated me. When asked if the tea and biscuits I had baked were to her liking, my friend, no doubt previously prompted by Nola, expressed reservations and I was told the only recourse was for me to be flogged in her presence. Which Nola did with unusual ferocity. I was made to bend across a chair a few inches away from where my friend sat, my dress was pulled up above my waist and my knickers pulled down to my knees, and I still remember every blow against my bare skin even now. When Nola had completed the punishment, she actually invited my friend to beat me likewise. Which she agreed to do, the damn traitor. I couldn't sit for days after that beating. I'm sure they had both planned this for ages.'

'You were going to tell me about the parties?'

'There were two sorts. Once or twice a month, Nola would have friends, mostly other women, sometimes couples for drinks in the evening. I would be made to serve. I recall now that this was already some time after the death of our parents in a car crash. We had both been left the whole estate but as I was still under-age, Nola had control of all the money.

Very often I would have to provide evidence of my servility and accept a flogging or the caress of the whip. The guests would seldom become involved. This was more a demonstration of Nola's power over me. At most, I would have to display my body for their after-drinks recreation, allow them to touch, twist my breast rings, provide evidence of my absolute docility and obedience.'

'What sort of people were these friends of Nola's?'

'Professional, middle-class, middle-aged, the women were lesbian or bisexual but she would never loan me to them. Their fun with me was restricted to the games with me on that particular evening.'

'The other parties?'

'They were more extreme. Infrequent also. I think I only attended five. Usually took place on Saturday nights and ran through the night. Never at the Regent's Park house Nola and I now shared, usually at plush residences somewhere outside London or in major provincial cities. I never knew where exactly we were, as I was blindfolded by Nola as we neared the locations.'

'Sounds frightening.'

'It was. Nola said I now had to prove that I was fully trained as a sub and these parties would be my final test. I was eager to prove her confidence in me was well-placed, and swore I would do everything I was told. It wasn't easy, but then I had little choice.'

'What sort of people attended these parties?'

'People like Nola. Genuine, experienced Masters. They were here to show off their slaves, male as well as female. We all wore collars and were forbidden to talk to each other as we were cuffed together awaiting our fate for the evening. Whatever happened to any of us, we were made to watch, and looking away would result in further punishment.'

'What happened to you?'

'Even now, I can't talk about many of the things that were done to me, or I was made to do to others.'

'What can you reveal?'

'Often the Masters would play games, make bets on us, pick cards for the humiliations that would be inflicted on us. A party night would seldom pass by without my not having been used in all holes by all the Masters present, male as well as female. On my first such party, my anal virginity was auctioned. I was blindfolded and made to kneel and suck every cock in the room, including the male slaves who were present. Unbeknown to me, the first one who managed to make me gag and retch would be designated to be the first to bugger me. I had successfully sucked three of the men and swallowed without heaving when I felt another place himself in front of my mouth and heard sniggers around the room. I knew something was wrong right there and then. A voice behind me remarked that I might require some help, and my hair was brutally pulled back and my head pushed forward onto the expectant cock. He was so heavily hung that the pressure applied to the back of my head forced me to swallow him and he was shoved all the way into my throat. I couldn't breathe. My lips were stretched to their fullest around its thickness and no air could pass from my lungs to my mouth. I couldn't help being sick all over him right there and then. It had been a set-up. He was one of the young slaves and his penis had elephantine proportions. At the next party, I was told he measured twelve inches or more.'

'Jesus!'

'I had no choice. After being made to clean up the mess I had caused, I was installed at the centre of the room as all watched and the young boy sodomised me. It hurt badly. I bled for days. I even fainted halfway through and had to be revived with smelling salts. They had no pity on me. When it was over and I stumbled back to the far wall, where the other slaves were grouped, I noticed Nola had not remained in the room for the dubious ceremony. One of the other girls, she was a tall, red-haired beauty with ever so pale skin, whispered to me that she had gone through the same ordeal. They always chose the pimply young slave boy with the enormous cock for a female slave's first experience of sodomy. Something about stretching us for further use. A Master saw her talking to me, chided her and announced this was one transgression too far. Could she not manage to keep her mouth closed long enough? Next time, she would be the one to be punished. She went paler than pale and tried to prevent her tears from flowing. I saw that she was terrorised. In the meantime, the young boy who had hurt me so much was now still the centre of attraction and being made to suck his own Master to hardness before he was made to kneel on all fours himself and his Master buggered him in turn.'

'How could you accept such things, Louise?'

'Because Nola ordered me to and I was in love with her.'

'The things we do for love...'

'I missed the next party. My anus was still bleeding days later and Nola had to take me to the doctor in Harley Street to have two stitches put in to repair me. The doctor just smiled when he examined me, as if he knew exactly which cock had done the damage. Nicely dilated, was all he commented upon, just right for the rest of us now.'

'He was an accomplice?'

'Yes, a founding member of their circle. When I had healed sufficiently, he was the first to take me in the arse at an ensuing party.'

'While you were being used by others at these parties, what did Nola do?'

'She liked to whip and torture the other Masters' female slaves. I once had to watch her fist another girl who appeared to be even younger than me. She had never, until then, done that to me. The poor kid screamed so much they had to gag her, but Nola's cruelty knew no bounds and she kept on twisting her hand and pounding the kid's innards to jelly.'

'You must have been scared by that.'

'Yes, but not so much as the day I had to watch the tall red-haired girl being punished. She had accumulated too many faults, according to her Master, and had to be made an example of. And all of us other slaves present were warned that if we even looked away one single second, a similar fate would befall us. It was awful.'

'What did they do to her?'

'She fought against them but she didn't stand a chance. It took four Masters to hold her down, while another brought in a huge dog...'

'No...'

'They placed her in the right position, kicked her legs apart and had the dog fuck her. Even now, I still have nightmares thinking of what I saw. Its paws scratched deep lines of blood across her back as it squatted over her and did the deed.'

'God!'

'That very moment, I swore I'd commit suicide if I ever allowed something like that to happen to me.'

'I can imagine.'

'Later, as the others played with the rest of us slaves, I saw her sobbing against the wall. They had connected her collar to the dog's leash and she sat there motionless while the animal greedily lapped up his own come which was still oozing out of her. I never saw her again. She was never brought to the other parties I attended, even though her erstwhile Master was present. Now, he had another woman.

'What can I say, Louise? And you were still only seventeen?'

'After that night, I think Nola began to sense my unease

about the sexual escalation in the relationship. A couple of days later, she stuck a Polaroid next to my bedside table. She had taken it when the red-haired girl was being violated by the dog. This was clearly a warning to me not to doubt her resolve and dare any form of disobedience to her will. But we only attended two more special Saturday night parties during the course of the following six months, and nothing more untoward than sex and whippings occurred, as if the group knew they had crossed a dangerous borderline. At the final party Nola took me to, I could somehow feel her distancing herself from me already, but I did not wish to acknowledge that a page was about to be turned. That night, the tall pimply young slave boy with the uncommon endowment came up for punishment and I was fitted with a strap-on and made to fuck him. I had never realised before I could switch from sub to becoming a most ferocious, vengeful dom. I plundered him with a vengeance. He also bled abundantly and I eventually had to be pulled off him by Nola. She had of course used a strap-on on me on many occasions, but we had never switched; she was not into penetration.'

'You said things were changing?'

'For some time, Nola had hinted that the present she was planning for my eighteenth birthday would be unforgettable. Two months prior to the event, she took me again to the doctor in Harley Street and my lips were pierced and the eight rings installed. I was told it would take some weeks to heal. Nola seldom used me in the weeks between my labial piercings, and often only returned home late with no word of explanation.'

'So what did she actually gift you with for your eighteenth birthday?'

'There was not even a greetings card in the morning. I slaved away in the kitchen all day and she came home around seven. She asked me to follow her to the bathroom, ordered me to undress, examined my rings and the now-fully healed piercings. I was told to close my eyes and felt her fit something across the rings. It was a special kind of safety pin which fits through both sets of four rings and closes with a miniature padlock, totally sealing the entrance to my vagina. There was a kind of beauty to it, this chastity device whose usefulness I couldn't quite understand. Later she explained to me that she had tired of me, wished to install a new friend in the house. By fitting me with the padlock she would still control me from a distance. I was to leave her house the following day! I was dumbstruck. I cried for hours.'

They spend their final day in Manhattan as normal lovers might.

They linger in bed, have breakfast sent up, touch, kiss, caress, talk about the weather.

He plans their day. They will lunch at a small Japanese sushi bar on the corner of Thirteenth and Sixth. She tells him she has never eaten raw fish before.

'You'll see,' he reassures her, 'it's nice.'

They catch a movie at the Angelika, trawl Tower Records for the obscure country and western CDs still missing from his extensive collection, explore the quaint streets of Alphabet City and end up with a final meal in a cajun joint close to the Flatiron Building. Oysters, gumbo and whatever entrée catches her fancy.

'Fattening me up, eh?' Louise remarks.

'Exactly, you're all bones and rings, my dear...'

He's not sure if she appreciates the joke.

'I'm off to shave.'

'OK.'

When he returns from the bathroom, her face is flushed. Her eyes shift when he looks at her, she appears guilty.

'What is it?' he asks.

'I've been bad.'

'How?'

'While you were washing, I touched myself.'

'So?'

'You didn't use me last night. I needed relief.'

'It's not a problem, Louise.'

'It's wrong for a slave to seek her own pleasure without the consent of her Master. You must punish me.'

His heart sinks.

So this is the way it is.

He handcuffs her to the bed post and arranges her nude body in the shape of an X across the soft green bed cover. She is not wearing the safety pin. As he widens the angle of her legs, her cunt gapes.

He hangs the 'Do Not Disturb' sign outside the door and leaves her in the room, captive, laid out like an offering, though not for the maid!

He loiters around reception until he finds a suitable man. A German tourist, wealthy-looking but with no taste in clothes. At first, the man does not take him seriously, but he insists. They share a coffee in the breakfast room. He explains. They do the deal. He gives the German the card key to their room.

He has no wish to watch.

'You have two hours,' he says. 'Be out of the room by then. She is handcuffed. I have the keys with me. She will not speak, or cry, or scream.'

'And I...?' asks the German, begging for confirmation of his dreams.

'She is totally yours. Anything you want.'

They are two of the slowest hours of his life. He walks four blocks north, then five blocks south. Peruses every window without even noticing their varied content.

When he finally returns, Louise is still handcuffed to the

bedpost, the taste of another man still leaking from her, dotting her stomach, her face, her breasts.

She smiles at him.

His slave.

That night, he sleeps badly, his mind in tumult.

Sunrise comes early, with a blanket of low clouds waltzing over the top of the highest skyscrapers.

He tells her about the dream.

In it, he has failed abysmally at becoming a Master and the only alternative is to become a slave himself. To stay with Louise, he sends a begging letter to Nola offering himself in exchange for further time with her. His pitiful demeanour makes her laugh but, as a game, she accepts.

Initially, she puts him on a diet, having no need of an over-weight slave. Then, when he becomes suitable she shaves his pubic hair and brands him, a large N carved into his buttocks. He is allowed to sleep in the same room as Nola and Louise, but on the floor, at the foot of their bed where he is forced to listen to their lovemaking and Louise's severe beatings. He is beaten too, made to wear an apron and serve their food; if ever he is caught with an erection he is whipped until he bleeds. But he is happy now, just living under the same roof as his companion of slavery. Eventually, he is allowed to attend the special parties where his role is to suck all the men to hardness before they fuck Louise, then to lick them clean after they have withdrawn from her orifices. In turn, she is to prepare the men who bugger him. He is no longer allowed to touch her, only to watch the increasing stations of her degra-dation. But the punishments get worse and worse, as he finds it impossible to repress his excitement as his cock invariably reacts shamelessly every time another man penetrates her.

Finally, the circle of Masters decrees the ultimate punish-ment at the next party he is to be brought to. Which is when he awoke.

'A companion in slavery,' Louise remarks. 'Yes, I think that would be quite appropriate for you...'

'Would it?'

'But it's all a dream, you know, Nola hates men, she would never want you as her slave. If you had a wife to offer in exchange for time with me, maybe then she might entertain your proposal. Dream on.'

'I will,' he says.

Q & A

'What did you do when Nola threw you out?'

'I pleaded, made a fool of myself, threw myself at her feet. Even begged to be retained if only as a servant, so that I might look after her and her new, young mistress.'

'Did you meet her, this new girl?'

'Yes, some months later. Tall, blonde, everything I wasn't. New. Virgin territory for Nola's cruel whims.'

'But she didn't allow you to stay on?'

'No. I was desperate. I thought she would never have me back. I had given up my studies without obtaining any diplomas or qualifications, how could I find a job, somewhere to live? Nola controlled my trust fund. During the two years I had spent with Nola I had deliberately lost the few friends I had before our encounter, I had nothing, I never even had any more normal clothes to wear. Nola had once mentioned, almost as a joke, a couple who had on two occasions visited her soirées and been witness to my servility and asked where they could find a similar maid. Maybe I could go and place myself in their service. The idea didn't appeal to me. Become a servant to people I had already privately served as a slave. But I had no other alternative. Nola phoned them and a deal was agreed.'

'And that's where you are now?'

'I've now worked here two years almost. They leave for

work – they are both senior managers for a large insurance company in a nearby town – early in the morning and my duties are to keep the house clean, wash, iron, dust, prepare the food. I am not allowed any mail or telephone calls. I play on the Internet. Watch TV. They are hard on me. The woman has custody of the padlock key, but she is capricious and often declines to set the rings free, particularly when I'm having my periods. It amuses her. Most of the time, I am just their servant, but sometimes they remember my nature and my past, usually when they have drunk heavily. He fucks me, she watches, has me lick her. Christmas last, I was seemingly too enthusiastic while he used me extensively and the next day, out of jealousy, she beat me badly.'

'Do you still hear from Nola?'

'Not often. She keeps in touch, though.'

'Do you still love her?'

'Yes, as much as ever.'

'Will she ever have you back?'

'I live in that hope, but I realise how unlikely it is. I'm realistic.'

'Are you happy?'

'Yes, in my own way. But living with my owners is boring. The house is in the middle of nowhere. The only contact I have with other human beings is when they take me on holiday with them. Spain in the summer; a house in the mountains in France at Easter. In Spain, I am allowed to wear shorts and bikinis. The padlock is taken off and I am allowed to be naughty. I fuck boys, with rubber protection of course. They don't mind as long as I'm not late back at their villa to cook the meals.'

'Can you see your life remaining the same for years to come, Louise? A leading question, I know.'

'I'm only twenty. I am a sub… But I don't wish to work for the Masters again. After New York, I might try somewhere else. It was whispered about at the parties sometimes, between subs, between our being used. It's a house. A sort of brothel. A house of punishment, for adepts of dominance and submission. In New Orleans. I might... I don't know... N once said I would be a pearl among inmates there. I've often dreamed of New Orleans. My grandfather came from there.'

'But N's the man who tried to brand you.'

'I know, but I think he would prove a good Master for me.... He's attuned to my nature.'

'It's your life.'

'It is.'

'And I'm no knight in shining armour, Louise. I have no mission in life to change your nature. You touch me, though. I feel much tenderness for you.'

'Do you think you could be my new Master, then?'

'I'm not sure. Willing to give it my best shot...'

'If you were a true dom, you would know already. I don't think you are somehow.'

'I'm sadly aware of the fact. But I still want to see you again. Badly. Please, Louise.'

His plea is an act of desperation.

'Maybe. Let me think.'

He packs.

He had asked the day before whether they should purchase a case for the clothes they had bought together, but she had declined. She came with nothing and insists she should return to her owners similarly. It would be suspicious otherwise and, unlike Nola's, she does not appreciate their beatings. He realises he has never even asked her what alibi, what lie she had used to justify her trip.

He watches as she stuffs the barely-worn chenille jumper, the rainbow skirt, the cream see-through blouse, the stockings and sundry knick-knacks into the hotel room's wicker waste basket. He's packed the cuffs and the strap-on in his own case, although he's thinking of disposing them in a washroom at the airport. It would be too embarrassing to be searched at customs.

They take the lift in heavy silence. He settles the bill with his credit card and the doorman hails a cab.

'Newark.'

It's early morning, ahead of the commuter traffic. The journey takes barely half an hour. Throughout, he holds her hand in his.

Way down his throat, there are a million words he wishes to say, but they break up like flotsam against the rampart of his lips. He knows he hasn't the eloquence to change her life. Or his.

Her flight is a whole hour earlier than his.

Her thin, fragile silhouette disappears down the neon-lit corridor that leads to her departure lounge. He has checked: her plane is on time. They haven't even said goodbye. Before the bend, she turns, smiles and blows him a kiss.

He knows he will never see her again. The e-mails will continue for a short time, then they will slow down and a day will come when she just disappears, the property of a new Master, who will forbid all contact with her former life. And his mind will imagine the worst. Violation. Torture. Death. Because the life she has chosen is a one-way street.

And his heart doesn't own the right passport.

8: Martin

I clicked on 'Save'. Then 'Save As'. Typed in 'Nola'. I had no printer with me, so the tale would have to stay inside the bowels of the laptop for the time being.

A veil of sadness descended upon me as I sat in the darkness, my eyes illuminated by the blue glow of the screen. I knew of Internet affairs of course. But somehow, the true nature of Louise and her unnamed, older lover resonated deep inside me and I felt for him, and for her dearly.

Now, I knew why Nola was so intent on finding her half-sister again. And the book had damn all to do with it.

Even though the hour was somewhat late, I rang Nola's hotel. It was time to talk, I'd decided. But she'd already checked out. It was child's play to follow her trail. She'd ordered a limousine airport service. The driver had dropped her at the United terminal at Kennedy. A quick browse through the schedules showed no direct flight to New Orleans, but a convenient connection in Raleigh-Durham.

At last, some of the pieces were beginning to fit.

But I was far from pleased to have been taken for a fool by Nola.

Actually, I was fuming. Maybe I would have to find Louise before she did.

9: Martin

The drunken revellers swarmed up and down Bourbon Street balancing their plastic cups of beer with alcoholic agility. On the wrought-iron balconies of the hotels and bars, even drunker punters looked down on the crowds below and offered gaudy beads to women who were sufficiently inebriated or liberated to flash their tits or more to the sound of much applause. In the early morning, there would be rivers of beer in the gutter which the city workers would hose away together with the massed detritus of the night before, an unholy mix of beads, crushed plastic, vomit and worse.

I moved away from the throng and met my local contact outside the Café du Monde. Two old black musicians were camped on the sidewalk and entertained the customers with old-fashioned jazz tunes, while tourists snapped away to their heart's content and kids gripped their animal-shaped balloons.

It appeared that Nola had settled in to the Dauphine Orleans Hotel, a stone's throw from Bourbon. And she was asking the same questions I was. Seeking Louise in the madness of the Vieux Carré, barely two weeks from Mardi Gras, when all hell would no doubt break loose across the city. She was not alone and he hadn't been able to identify her male companion, a tall grey-haired man of European appearance. The room was registered in her name only.

But there was no trace of her younger sister.

I thanked my contact for the meagre scrap of information and handed him a hundred dollar bill. He was an ex-policeman, still plugged in to the local zeitgeist and eager to help.

'Is there much of an S&M scene?' I asked Neil.

'This is the Big Easy,' he answered. 'Every scene you can think of and more is present, and generously available.'

I smiled. Persisted.

'We'd be talking of something very illegal. Not just a run of the mill brothel, with a smidgen of corporal punishment, a show to entertain the clients. Real stuff, pain, serious stuff?'

'I can think of a few establishments. But they are very private. Have to be,' he said. 'But they're out of my reach. The protection is much higher up. Couldn't help you gain access.'

'Names will do. And whereabouts. I'd take it from there.'

He scribbled a few lines on one of the paper serviettes and slid it over to me.

'Can't help you if anything goes wrong, though,' Neil added. 'These places are way beyond my scope. I'd be careful, if I were you, Jackson. And do keep my name out of it, please. I'd appreciate that.'

I nodded my understanding.

Around Jackson Square the portrait artists and palm readers were packing up their stalls and young goths lazed around on the steps of the church, all pale skin and heavy kohl make-up, like vampires awaiting the fall of night.

I treated myself to an oyster po'boy at the Napoleon House and lost myself in the wake of the crowds of increasingly noisy tourists and sidewalk tap dancers, my steps punctuated by the conflicting cross-rhythms of the bands in the open-door bars on each side of the street. Blues fighting country wrestling with rock duelling with dixie, a whole symphony of loud syncopation in full, heavy flow.

I'd investigate the S&M joints the following day.

Back in my room at the unfashionable hotel on Burgundy Street, I called up Nola. Felt like confronting her. She, and her male companion, were not in. I didn't bother to leave a message. It would have been rude anyway.

The following morning, to keep him off my back while I concentrated on the Poshard sisters case, I mailed Christopher Streetfield. I didn't promise any results in the ongoing search for his wife, just wanted to keep him on the hook. I was certain that whoever had jumped me in Amsterdam had nothing to do with his job; the file must have been stolen by mistake. There was no other explanation. Who else would want the photographs of Kay and the addresses and telephone numbers of her few girlfriends from university days? It must be a coincidence and I couldn't allow my mind to linger over it.

I cased the clubs Neil had told me about in the morning. The Magnetic Fields just felt wrong somehow; as I watched its doors from the window of a nearby bar where I was nestling an espresso, I caught sight of a couple of cleaners about to enter it and quickly approached them. Pretexted I was interested in joining and just wanted to see what the inside looked like. They hesitated but a few greenbacks soon changed their mind and I was allowed a quick peep. There was something awfully vulgar about the place, lush carpets on floors and strung across walls, deep leather seats. This was no place of danger or transgression, more like a swingers' club for tired executives. It was just a pumped-up strip club from all appearances.

I mentally crossed it off my list. Surely Louise had better taste, or more of a death wish.

The Moby Lounge was a different kettle of fish altogether. From the outside, it just looked like another French Quarter villa with a leafy garden behind its gates obscuring the view of the house beyond. It was at the wrong end of Bourbon, well beyond the noise and the gay zone, almost at Ramparts level. It screamed discretion. More than just another gentleman's club where things might sometimes get out of hand. Could this be the house Louise had alluded to, unless her lover had fictionalised their encounter and its attendant dialogue?

I resolved to return here that night, when the place opened.

But I still had a whole day to waste and no wish to do the obligatory bayou and crocodile tour on the Creole Queen riverboat, let alone visit the Aquarium of the Americas.

Around lunch hour I stationed myself close to the Dauphine Orleans. Sure enough, I soon caught Nola Poshard and her tall escort leaving the hotel. She looked stunning, her legs flowing forever under the thin material of her red taffeta skirt. I followed them a few blocks and saw them take a seat for lunch at Tujague's on Decatur. Perfect. I knew the place from a previous visit to the Crescent City and there was no way they'd be out of here for at least 90 minutes. I rushed back to their hotel.

Gaining access to their room was child's play. Chambermaids are always leaving their carts unattended in hotel corridors and, as I expected, a set of pass-keys was handily hanging from a door on the next floor up while the maid went in search of the extra hand towels I requested. I carefully slipped a single key off the ring and walked up the service stairs to Nola Poshard's floor.

They had not been sleeping together and both double beds showed signs of having been slept in. This was no surprise. I quickly rifled through drawers and luggage but failed to find anything interesting or at any rate relevant. Damn. Nola's selection of underwear certainly had its aesthetic charms, but anyone could have told me that from just looking at the way she walked and behaved. I was about to draw a line under this ill-thought venture into my current employer's privacy when, force of habit, I slipped a hand inside the jacket the tall guy had left draped over one of the chairs by the door to the bathroom.

What I found gave me a start.

The photographs of Christopher Streetfield's wife.

Definitely the very same that had disappeared in Amsterdam.

Curiouser and curiouser. And damn worrying. My mind in overdrive, I raced through every possible connection.

There were none that made sense.

Apart from one: Nola knew the truth – I was the connection.

A wind of panic blew through me.

I just couldn't see how they knew.

It was impossible.

My breath resumed its normal status.

I put the photographs back in the inside pocket of the jacket where I had found them. I had no need for them, so there was no need to advertise the fact I'd been in the room by retrieving them.

There was no one in the corridor. I crept out of the room and took the elevator down to the lobby, leaving the stolen pass-key in an ashtray.

I spent the afternoon putting every fact of the case, the two cases, under my mental microscope, puzzling through every step I had taken since that first day in London, the words I'd said, the people I'd seen, spoken to, fucked, been fucked by, squeezing every fact I could retrieve every which way, but still the whole picture just refused to settle into a simple, comprehensible pattern.

I must have dozed off briefly, my mind a total blank. As ever, it was an interlude of bad dreams, and ghosts. Ghosts? Who was I kidding but myself? One ghost.

When I snapped out of my lethargy, I immediately saw the envelope that had been slipped under my door.

It had been written by a woman. Elegant, cursive letters, with surprisingly square o's and a's. Educated.

It said we appeared to be searching for the same thing and suggested we join forces. Between 6 and 8 at the Firebird on Toulouse. I was to look for a small tattoo of a gun. There was no signature. Just the letter C.

From where I sat, just a few feet away from the stage where she danced, the stripper appeared strikingly tall and towering from the elevated position where she gyrated, if not particularly voluptuous, but what she lacked in breasts she more than made up in assurance and supple grace.

She had begun her set as I entered the anonymous club where a few men were quietly sipping their five dollar drinks and trying to avoid the eyes of the other punters for fear of recognition. A matronly waitress navigated between the sparse tables prompting the reorders.

I had unashamedly placed myself at the table nearest the stage and could count every speck of dust still lingering here and there on the shiny surface of the dance area.

The girl on stage had begun her moves to a slow, melancholy Bruce Springsteen song, bathed in the heart of a solitary red-weakening-to-pink electric spot which highlighted her body against the diffuse darkness of the club's recesses. Next to her, a shiny metal pole anchored the stage to the club's low ceiling.

She was already partly undressed. Just wore a black bikini ensemble which contrasted sharply with the deep white of her skin. No high heels or stockings or other accoutrements of the skin trade. Her movements were steady and measured as she milked every nuance of the drowsy melody, each curve of her body losing itself in the hypnosis of the music, espousing the languid rhythm. She didn't even look at the audience, her eyes distant and focused on the world inside her, no come-on, no invitations for further tips, as if totally indifferent to the sordid environment she navigated through as she danced. But

she was sexy, I had to admit. Rather. As she turned and
turned, her regal arse strained against the thin material of her
bikini bottom and every minor tremor of her leg and thigh
muscles seemed to lead back, to end in a tremulous movement
in the very apex of her crotch. But still her face showed no
emotion as she lost herself in the music.

The girl had class. She was a stripper not a teaser. Others
would have begun their set shielded in a layer of gaudy, so-
called sexy outer clothing and built the desire with every
shedding of garment, promising more with every discarded
item. This young woman was saying 'Here I am; this is what I
am; I'm tall and skinny and white as porcelain and my tits are
just an A or B cup but I have a great butt and you can pay and
watch but can't touch and I enjoy what I do and live in a
world that's much better than yours, so there'.

The music segued into an REM tune and, without ceremony, she undid the clasp of her top, allowed it to float to the
floor and quickly revealed her breasts, all pale, pink, soft
nipples, and her left hand gripped the metal pole and she
gracefully propelled herself into a full-circle revolution with
both feet just a few inches off the ground, came down again
and resumed her gentle sway to the music. Her small breasts
were firm, high, and didn't even move or shake during the
rapid manoeuvre. Nice. Now, her body began flexing as she
hastened the dance in unison with Michael Stipe's anguished
accents, her strong pelvis now the very centre of her exertions.

I looked around at the other punters. Some spoke, others
watched, but none seem to take any notice of the fact that this
stripper was out of the ordinary. She leaned backwards, her
crotch stretching against the fabric. Resumed her upwards
position and then leaned forward, cupping her breasts in both
hands and teasing the nipples. Standard moves from the
manual but ones she managed to accomplish with a total

absence of vulgarity or titillation. If she'd been wearing a garter or moved nearer to the edge of the stage, as others invariably did, I would have slipped her a few dollar bills with great pleasure, in appreciation of her skill and attitude, but she remained glued to the centre of the dance area, always within reach of the metal pole, swaying, dancing; I even thought I heard her humming along to the tune under her breath. A patina of breaking sweat now covered her upper body, emphasising the glitter she had conservatively sprinkled over herself earlier, every shiny eye capturing my imagination, lodged in the curve of her neck, dusted thinly over the valley of her breasts and then, daringly, almost as a line, an arrow from her navel to the still uncharted, unknown area shielded by her black bikini pants, like a promise of dark desire in her most private parts.

The song came to an end. The tape jumped and the third and final tune of her set began.

A small group of football fans wearing the Bordeaux colours of their team had entered the club and now sat to my right. Noisily ordered their drinks. Made a disparaging remark about the stripper's lack of frontal assets.

I turned my attention back to her.

The plaintive accents of an Aimée Mann song.

Once again with no sense of theatrics, the blonde on stage removed her final piece of clothing and I held my breath as her body reintegrated the private country of the music, and she began to sway, her long legs rooted to the ground, held ever so apart, like a fragile tree in the wind. The storm rose and the branches of her limbs embraced the motion, her head rolling a little as she wavered, fully exposed in the glare of the spotlight.

As the lingering song reached its chorus, the stripper slowly moved, for the very first time, to the edge of the stage, right in front of where I sat, her cunt level with my eyes. She was shaven, the darker, discreet line of her gash like a forgotten scar on the surface of her Barbie crotch. A nicely plump pudenda incongruously highlighted by the arrow of glitter. The blonde crouched. The top of her body shivered along to the strains of the rock 'n'roll beat of the song. I couldn't help my gaze following the downward move of her crotch as she squatted. Her cunt gaped open, revealing a scarlet darkness. Her hands caressed her upper body with deliberate slowness and then finally lowered themselves and momentarily shielded her cunt, just as my eyes had caught a glimpse of shiny moistness, like an infinitely thin spider web connecting her stretched-apart labia. I looked up into her eyes and took a direct hit. She was watching my reaction. Strong, brown eyes that seemed to delve deep into me. We were now caught in a grip of recognition. A contact. As if we were the only two people present here and the rest of the audience and the surroundings didn't even exist. Just the stripper, the music and me. It had become a private show.

Her hands drew away from her cunt lips, lingering ever so daringly over them as if she were actually going to open herself up completely and reveal her innards.

She drew herself up from her squatting position and straightened her body again. Her movements quickened as the finale approached and the drum and bass punctuated the acceleration of the song's rhythm. But still inches away from my eyes.

I pulled myself away from the enticing contemplation of her displayed cunt.

Close to her gash, on the border of her shaven pudenda, there was a small dark patch. I squinted and it came into focus.

A tattoo. Of a gun.

The music faded away as the blonde's dance turned motionless and the spotlight hiccuped away from her.

There was scattered applause, and in the penumbra I watched her bend to pick up her abandoned garments.

'A nice round of applause for this very special performance from our New York guest Cornelia!' some compere said over the scratchy sound system. 'Time to reorder, guys. In a few minutes, we have the popular Charmaine...'

We met outside the bar and walked two blocks in silence to a quiet Starbucks. Cornelia wore a simple white short-sleeved T-shirt and jeans. In the open air, I could see the natural features of her face were as untouched by superfluous make-up as they were on the stage. No one could have guessed she was a stripper now.

Just lipstick, a soft, warm shade of red against the unnatural pallor of her skin. This was a woman who didn't spend much leisure time in the sun.

She set her bulging shoulder bag down on the floor by the table.

'So...' I said.

'We meet,' she said, in answer to my unformulated question.

'The gun tattoo came as a surprise, I must say.'

Cornelia smiled.

'A present to myself after my last job.'

'It's different, I admit.'

'Yes, so much less vulgar than a flower, a rose or whatever most gals would have there. Don't you think?'

'I've been hearing a bit about you over the last few weeks.'

'Have you? Not all bad, I hope?'

'I'm not sure. Sometimes second-hand rumours can prove confusing.'

She ordered an iced tea.

'I know you're seeking Louise Poshard,' Cornelia calmly stated.

'I guessed so.'

'So am I.'

'Really?'

'I even guess we have the same paymaster. They can be such a nuisance, can't they? They never trust anyone to do the job properly.'

'An interesting assumption.'

'And we both guess she might be in hiding at the Moby Lounge, don't we?'

'At this point, I should ask you how you've arrived at such a conclusion,' I said, enjoying this sparring game with Cornelia. 'But maybe I shouldn't insult your intelligence. Some of my contacts actually told me you can prove dangerous, so I shall carefully refrain from doubting you.'

I watched the quiet smile spread across her perfect lips.

'Dangerous? Little me? Well, I do wonder how?'

'You've a body and a way of dancing well capable of provoking a heart attack in the unprepared,' I ventured.

'You liked?' Cornelia asked.

'Very much,' I admitted.

'Good. It's nice to feel attractive. But I dislike mixing business and pleasure, Martin,' she added.

Where had I heard that before? Nola Poshard. What was this, a surfeit of femmes fatales?

'You're not my type anyway,' I lied.

She ignored this.

'I just thought it would be useful to meet. I think we can help each other.'

'Can we?'

'Tonight, you were maybe planning going to the Moby Lounge?'

'Correct.'

'You wouldn't gain entrance. I've checked. Very strictly members only, I fear.'

'I see. Can't say that surprises me, what with some of the likely goings on inside.'

'Strong stuff?'

'That's the story. S&M stuff.'

'Oh. That would explain why the people here couldn't get me admittance, even as a ...working girl. Had no contacts.'

'I suspect the Moby Lounge entertainment is strictly in-house, not hired in,' I said.

Cornelia frowned.

And for just an instant it made her look vulnerable, her brown eyes clouding, her mind racing in overdrive, her gaze faraway. I almost saw the child Cornelia had once been.

Which, incongruously, redirected my own thoughts towards the now-so-distant Aida. And my heart gently skipped a beat. Where was she now? Back in the cramped Dutch coastline cottage, or on a train towards Amsterdam or at another bar in another hotel, waiting for the right man, about to take her hesitant step into whoredom? My material girl.

The thought passed quickly and I was back in New Orleans.

'There might be a way the two of us could gain access to the Moby Lounge. Easier as a couple,' Cornelia said.

'Tell me.'

'I know someone, back in New York, who could effect an introduction. But we'd have to assume a role, blend in with the scene,' she continued.

'I'd be game,' I told her. I already knew there was no way I could get in there on my own. I wouldn't fit. With this curious young woman it might well prove possible. But deep inside I also knew her agenda wasn't the same as mine.

She buried her hand inside her purse.

'Do you have any quarters?' she asked me.

I found a handful.

She rose from her chair, unbelievably slim and towering, the fabric of her thin, white T-shirt straining against the silhouette of her hard nipples, her tight jeans clinging to the moody curves of her arse. I sighed. She made her way to the washroom where our waiter had advised her the telephone was.

I sipped slowly on my espresso, my teeth a sieve between the syrupy streams of sugar I had drowned in the coffee and the bitter harshness of the concentrate.

Cornelia returned five minutes later.

'I think it'll work,' she said. 'I have to phone back in an hour for confirmation.'

I nodded silently.

'People who know people who know people, you know,' she said.

'Working in the sex industry has it perks, I see,' I said.

'It's only part-time,' Cornelia answered. 'A gal has to make a living, pay for the bare necessities.'

'You've been stripping long?' I asked her. I had never known strippers before, but nonetheless she didn't fit the preconceived mould. Not just the way she looked, danced, but the attitude, the voice. She was in category of her own.

She ignored my question.

'We have an hour or so to kill,' she said.

'I can think of worse things,' I feebly joked. But then I've never been your private eye who is also a knight of the mean streets and can crack a quip at the drop of a whiskey glass. Don't misunderstand me, I have a sense of humour alright, it just works with a time delay.

This naturally drew a blank look from Cornelia.

'Another coffee or two or three?' I suggested.

'Nah,' she said. 'I need some fresh air. Been cooped up indoors too long.'

We walked out of the Starbucks.

Onto Magazine Street, tourists ambling along, idling time away outside the antique-shop windows while musicians and puppeteers displayed their wares on every street corner.

We were wary of each other and the aimless walk through the Vieux Carré was full of silences. Something about the way she walked, her stance, reminded me somehow of Kay. As ever, the memories brought an anguished knot to the heart of my guts. Chin forward, whole body in languorous pursuit. Rather distinctive. She appeared more interested by the displays of the few used bookstores we came upon, or the prints in the photographic gallery. Jewellery and clothes didn't seem to interest her much.

She ignored point blank all my questions about her interest in Louise Poshard and I felt at a disadvantage. She appeared to know so much about me and why I was here in New Orleans, while she remained an enigmatic if savagely sensual enigma. I had been dealt the wrong pack of cards and even my old poker skills were of no use to me here.

An hour passed.

Full of question marks and a state of uneasiness and apprehension.

There was bank of telephones just past the lobby of the Bourbon Sonesta, to the right of the oyster bar. With a nod, Cornelia indicated I should wait for her amongst the disembarking tourists.

She stayed away almost fifteen minutes. Halfway through her absence, fearing she might have given me the slip, I peered around the corner at the wall of telephone alcoves and spied her speaking calmly on one of them and jotting down notes on a piece of paper.

'It's on,' she told me upon returning to the hustle and bustle of the crowded lobby.

'Great.'

'Tomorrow night,' she added. 'That's when the next party

occurs. We've been recommended. Serious East Coast practitioners of the dark arts,' Cornelia smiled mischievously. 'Think you can pull it off?'

'I'm sure you will prove of invaluable assistance in the matter.'

'So who plays sub?' she asked me.

'Not sure I can picture myself on a leash,' I said.

'Yes, I suppose dom is easier to impersonate,' Cornelia replied. 'I'll play sub, then.'

'You're the artist. Shouldn't stretch you,' I jested.

'Just games, Mr Jackson,' she said.

'Am I expected to play Master in full leather regalia?' I asked her.

'I don't think the Moby Lounge is into that. I'd suggest you just wear your usual all-black. Maybe add a tie, say? Will make you look more elegant, forceful, no?' Cornelia winked at me.

'And you?'

'I'll find what I need on Bourbon. Just a few touches to add to a work outfit.'

'Oh, yes,' I said. I'm sure she had a varied and most interesting *garde-robe*.

We made arrangements to meet in twenty-four hours or so. Cornelia declined my invitation to gumbo and oysters at the Red Fish Grill.

She faded into the street crowds, as much as someone so striking can ever fade. Their image stays in your mind. For a very long time indeed.

After my meal, I made another visit to her strip club. I was now keen to see her at work (or was it play?) again now that I knew her slightly better. OK, so I wanted to see her body again. Those small tits that just beckoned for the caress of a distracted finger, those long legs that went on forever, the ever so crooked front tooth that appeared whenever she half-opened her lips whilst dancing in a parody of lust, the strategically-placed tattoo, that cunt. But the other girls paraded one after the other as the evening grew old and no sign of Cornelia. I asked and was told she no longer worked there.

Back in my room, images of Cornelia taunted my imagination and I relieved myself by hand. Maybe it was tiredness or the grief I was still carrying, but the flesh on the screen of my imagination, the skin so white, so cold, all spun around, flesh like a whirlpool, pictures of Kay crying, of Aida's mole, all effortlessly merging with Cornelia's dance of desire.

I came.

And with it, the guilt.

In torrents.

10: The truth and nothing but the truth (or, Another Story)

He sees her at a party at the Brighton Pavilion. A cocktail party sponsored by a Rupert Murdoch-owned publishing house. Chardonnay, orange juice, stale peanuts and crisps.

Her frizzy hair like a Medusa head, all wild blonde curls fighting a losing battle against the forces of tidiness. Her gawky walk, like a rare animal not quite used to her body's equilibrium, long tentative strides across the party floor, a glass and a plate balanced in her left hand as she moves from group to group, both confident and shy.

Who is she, he wonders.

He's in town for the day, has been invited to give a small talk to the Crime Writers' Association Conference about the realities of the private investigator's life in today's Britain. He's preceded by a retired customs officer who debunks smuggling, and is followed by a pathologist with a case full of gory slides, who will attract ten times the amount of questions. The audience carefully takes notes. They are mostly middle-aged women with blue rinses who think writing about crime is jolly entertaining.

Hello, he introduces himself.

Oh yes, she remembers him. She was in his audience, didn't he see her, at the back towards the right of the hotel function room? He hadn't. Maybe it was the spotlights shining in his eyes. He is sure she would have stood out. He apologises.

She is talking to a retired police inspector from Nottingham. He is not sure whether the boring man is also here as some sort of adviser or has actually turned to writing mystery books in the wake of his retirement. He gathers she works as a junior editor for a small, independent London publishing house. Has been asked to set up a new crime list and is cruising for authors and contacts.

He nods and mumbles and never really joins the conversation. The room is noisy. He notes her eyes are brown and her skin has a milky pallor against which her wild hair stands out in striking contrast. He's sure the colour is natural but the curls must be the result of a perm. But you don't ask about things like that in public, do you?

The party breaks up and the crowd disperses to return to the hotel where the talks are continuing. Someone asks him a question and she moves on. He loses track of her. Later, she is not in attendance.

It's the conference's last night.

He sees her again at the bar in the evening, she smiles a hello of recognition but is already too busy with other interlocutors and he can't draw her away.

He gives up and opts for an early night. Watches a softcore sex film on the pay channel. It's so tame he has difficulties achieving an erection.

He is up early for breakfast. Leaving the hotel's restaurant he notices her, hair still dishevelled in wondrous splendour, sitting in one of the armchairs in the reception area, dressed in a blue dress with small white polka dots. Her left bra strap is visible over the soft contour of her shoulder. Black.

People are queuing up to settle their bills.

He walks over to her, greets her.

Morning.

She looks up from reading a Sara Paretsky paperback.

Oh hello.

It was nice talking.

Yes, she agrees.

But they never did manage a proper conversation, did they?

So, back to London?

Yes, she nods, they exchange a meaningless glance and she closes the paperback shut.

For a brief moment, he feels shy like an eighteen-year old courting the belle of the ball.

Are you catching the 10.05?

No, I'm being picked up.

I see. Pity...

Yes, she agrees.

Someone calls over to him. He excuses himself; it's just someone wishing to exchange business cards. When he looks back, she is already gone.

On the train back to Waterloo, he reads the Sunday newspapers. But she is on his mind.

A strange awkward beauty emanated from her, there was the faint trace of a scar on her cheek and he wonders how she got it. Wore no make-up save for a deep pink shade of lipstick. She attracts him.

Two mornings later in his Holborn office, he pulls out the conference programme and looks up the membership list. Yes, there she is listed alongside the name of the company she works for. He obtains the telephone number from inland directory enquiries.

Remember me?

Oh yes, you were interesting.

Really? I'm pleased I made an impression.

He knows she is smiling.

I was wondering...?

Yes?

Maybe we could meet for a drink? Talk?

He feels the smile broaden. Maybe she was expecting him
to call?

Yes. Why not?

We never did have a chance down in Brighton, did we?

That's true, she agrees.

The knot in his stomach loosens.

We can talk about crime, she continues.

Yes. It's a vast subject.

A lot to talk about.

Indeed.

He finds out her offices are in Goodge Street so they are
fairly close to each other. Her lunch hours are somewhat busy
for the rest of the week, she has this horror novel to copy-edit
which has been delivered late and it's her only chance to catch
up. Why not Friday evening. A pub off the Charing Cross
Road. Six-fifteen?

He readily agrees to the time and place.

Two nights before, he is idling the evening away at his flat
leafing through all the magazines he has somehow accumulated over the last few months and not yet read. One of them
features a portfolio of nudes by the American photographer
Gerard Malanga. A photograph, a woman nude in three-
quarters view by a window, her face in darkness, her hair
turned into a halo of light by the sun outside the window,
catches his attention. The body shape he reckons could be
hers. The black and white emphasises the nude woman's
pallor and she has strong hips. Yes, it could well be her. This
time, the erection comes easily.

She arrives on time and, not without difficulty they find a
free table in the basement bar. The noise is deafening, all the
Soho bright young things and office wannabes chattering
away, screaming for attention at the outset of the week-end,
and the jukebox itself drowned by their frantic conversations.

She wears a white blouse and jeans.

Have you ever been to America? he asks her. The photograph of the nude woman at the window has burned a deep hole in his libidinous mind. It's a chance in a million but he's not about to ask her if she has ever posed nude.

No, but I've always wanted to. But there's never been time, or the financial wherewithal. You?

Yes, often. I love it, find it so fascinating a place, you know.

I imagine it must be.

So, finished your copy-editing?

She has.

He asks her about the book.

The way she describes it, the novel sounds interesting, a tale full of sound, fury, incest and stranded birds on a northern shore. It's her first purchase as an editor and she has a strong belief in it. The author's previous two books for other publishers were commercial failures but she hopes this one, with her editorial input, will be a breakthrough (it won't: the reviews will prove decent but the sales abysmal, he will find out later).

She asks him how he became a private detective. Tells him he doesn't look the type.

He informs her he left his dirty trench coat, dark glasses and rolled-up copy of yesterday's *Times* back at the office with his secretary whose name is Velda.

The joke raises a laugh.

She has a few crooked teeth and this imperfection in her just blows him away.

The first half hour races by full of a hundred things unsaid. By now, every word they say to each other over the din can be heard clearly, in contrast to the opening minutes of the dialogue when so much had to be repeated over the background noise of the pub. Her eyes shine. The perfume she is wearing wafts towards him at irregular intervals, a smell he knows he will always associate with her thereafter. Green flowers, a touch of musk, a hint of perspiration and fresh soap.

They finally reach their first silence.

He gets another round of drinks.

So what did you wish to talk about? she asks him, snapping him out of a whirlpool of confused and contradictory thoughts.

I didn't realise we hadn't been talking, he smiles back at her.

You know what I mean.

Do I?

Unless you have a book project you want to pitch to me, and I don't flatter myself there were editors at the conference with a much bigger purse for the right project, I don't think you called me to discuss crime and its sundry implications, somehow.

You're right.

He knows it's time to come clean.

I just wanted to see you. Something about you, the way you talk, you walk, all those clichés. Damnit... I find you awfully attractive.

I thought so, she answers.

The response could have been worse. She could have laughed, walked off, slapped him, or just said no, you pitiful man.

I hadn't realised my lust was so obvious. Or have you taken classes in reading body language?

Actually, my company has published a book on the subject. But I haven't read it, I must confess. Terrible of me, no?

A glimmer of apprehension rises in his gut.

Her eyes look down deep inside him.

Estimating.

Weighing.

Judging him.

The sort of examination he sadly knows he can't sustain indefinitely.

He breaks the ice.

So where does that uncomfortable declaration leave us? Or me? he asks her.

The silence between them stretches over a few seconds and it feels like a whole century of indecision

I'm married, you know, she finally says.

William Tell in drag deliberately missing the apple and going straight for his heart.

I didn't know.

The fool in him hadn't even bothered to look down at her hand. And the now obvious wedding ring.

I see, is all he can force himself to answer.

But I'm flattered by your attentions, she continues.

And flattery will get me nowhere, he suspects.

There are moments when you know silence is the worst option on offer. If he said nothing right now or just 'sorry' he realises they will part in a few minutes with platitudes and that would be that. He forces himself to say something, anything.

So... how long have you been married? he asks her.

Seven years, she replies.

You must have been young.

The year following university.

What does he do? He almost asks what the 'lucky man' does, but doesn't.

Journalist. Financial and business. For a press agency.

I see.

She lowers her eyes.

He takes me for granted, she volunteers.

He seizes the safety line and immediately changes the subject.

They spend another hour in the pub basement. Small talk. He admits he's not much of a drinker.

Are you in a hurry? he asks her.

Not really, she says. Don't have to be home until ten or even a bit later.

He suggests they eat.

She accepts.

After the meal, they retrieve his car from the underground car park below Bloomsbury Square and he drives her to Charing Cross station. He's willing to take her all the way to south London but she's happy to catch the train. Blocked in traffic in Trafalgar Square, his left hand rests on the hand brake. Silently, she moves her own hand over and gently touches his. He drops her on the Strand, outside the station.

He calls her at work the next day.

Another drink?

I don't mind.

They meet in the bar of a large West End hotel. It's quieter. They share a couch. He can feel the heat from her body. Is hypnotised by her hair. Tries to count every wild curl on her head.

It's difficult, she says, I like you too.

She allows him to caress her neck, distractedly twirl some of the loose curls hanging there against the milky white of her skin.

They part around eleven. He feels hollow and the look in her eyes speaks of quiet despair.

On Monday, he rings her.

I want you, he says.

I know, she calmly replies.

I want to sleep with you.

Another early evening bar in another anonymous hotel, leather furnishings, barman with slicked back hair, a background of soft whispers isolating them from the world around.

They exchange sexual histories and intimate confidences. Their glasses are now empty.

Come, he says.

They walk the half-mile to his office block.

He unlocks the suite.

In the darkness, they kiss.

Hands everywhere.

The infinitely soft cushion of her breasts, the imprint of her teeth scraping against his invading tongue, bodies grinding against each other.

Your hands are so warm, she remarks as he explores the landscape of her flesh.

She catches her breath before the renewed onslaught of his lips.

Soon they are both dishevelled, his shirt open, her fingers brushing the hairs on his chest, raking his front, her blouse open and her bra unclipped, the pink aureolae of her small breasts on fire from the savaging of his tongue and delicate teeth, her tights rolled down to her knees, the humidity from her sex staining the front of her white knickers.

They surface for air.

She glances at her watch. It's already past ten.

I really must go, she says.

What did you tell him you were doing? he asks.

She straightens her clothing.

He's on a later shift, she says. Won't be home until eleven at the earliest. He'll be so tired he'll just walk in and slump on the bed.

Good, he says. He would hate the idea of her husband fucking her tonight. She had earlier revealed that she prefers to be taken in a doggie position and the image tortures his mind. Will keep him awake all night.

He has to go to Manchester on a case the following day and when he finds the time to call her office he discovers she is in a meeting. He doesn't leave a message. And then it's the week-end. Three days out of touch.

During which time he tries to imagine all the things she might be doing. Cooking, dusting their flat, shopping, seeing a movie, peeling potatoes, reading. But all that stays in his mind is her husband's cock ploughing her with vulgar vigour. Is she a moaner? A quiet one?

He receives her letter in Monday's first mail. Just as he is about to call her.

They have gone too far, she writes. It's wrong. All very wrong. Maybe they should stay apart. Maybe meet up in a few months, just as good friends, you know.

Damn, she has had second thoughts.

He writes her a letter in which he summons all his powers of persuasion. By the end of the week, she has not answered. He writes another. Two weeks pass by. All he can think of is her, and the Amazon-like grace of her lanky body. A letter a day. He surprises himself by finding new words, new things to say, every time he puts pen to paper.

Please, he says. Change your mind. Give me a chance. Give us a chance. Just once. She had, in conversation, revealed past occasional thoughts of adultery with other men she had come across, passes made which she had turned down. She has always been faithful. I am not just another man is what he is trying to say.

It's been ages since he has wanted a woman the way he wants her.

She phones.

Enough letters, she says. We have to talk.

The next evening. The bar of the same hotel. Usual time.

Yes, he says.

He's already sitting when she arrives, her customary gin and orange awaiting her on the small table. She appears distant.

He apologises for the bombardment of letters. Explains how strongly he feels for her, how he realises he is asking her too much, how if it never happens she will always wonder at the back her mind how it would have been, a self-serving and cowardly argument he recognises, how this, how that, and....

I will, she suddenly says.

What? he says.

He doesn't understand.

I will sleep with you, she says.

The trapdoor under his stomach opens and he plunges in headfirst.

They make arrangements.

Neither of them wishes to succumb to vulgarity, no office floor or flea-pit hotel for their affair. Not for their first time together, at any rate.

Somewhere discreet, they decide. Outside London.

They become lovers a fortnight later. It's a Tuesday morning. In an airport hotel, the distant rumbling of planes taking off or landing barely audible through the plate glass windows. He finally unveils her cunt and its forest of darker blonde curls is in harmony with the jungle of her hair. He sighs. Kisses her warmth, his tongue slowly parting her labia and tasting her for the first time. Strong, salty, intoxicating.

He retreats. She takes a step back and lies down on the bed. He approaches the intimate geography of her genitals, quietly opens her with all the delicacy his fingers can muster. Her insides are coral pink, ready to explode. He invades her with his mouth. She widens the angle of her legs. He is kneeling by the foot of the bed, still dressed, now installed between her thighs.

He nibbles, licks, pulls and chews her inner folds, searching for the nerve ends of her pleasure, and soon her heartbeat speeds up and tremors pass through her body, shaking his soul as the electricity moves imperceptibly from her redness through to his tongue.

Finally, she cries out.

I want you inside me. Now!

He quickly undresses and holding his cock in one hand to guide its entrance path, he enters her.

The threshold of adultery is so easy to cross.

She is not a moaner.

Neither is she totally silent.

With every few thrusts, she just whispers 'Jesus', 'Jesus,' as he pumps into her and the volcano of her loins radiates its implacable heat, their skin incandescent and wet, fingers digging into rumps, scratching, holding on to each other with the energy of despair.

They have become lovers.

The affair will last ninety days.

The lovemaking that first morning stretches well into the afternoon. They exhaust each other, always eager for more, avid for further sensations, as if throwing away one at a time the shackles of their previous lives in a frenzy of desire.

He takes a shower. Returns to the room. She is lying on the bed, obscenely spreadeagled on the cover, her cunt still gaping open from his assaults and leaking his come, raw, lips swollen from the blood rush and all the friction. He stands watching her beauty in such wonderful disarray. She opens her eyes, sees him and beckons. He moves nearer and she takes his cock in her mouth and soon revives him.

Finally spent, it's now mid-afternoon, they share a bath and he traces hieroglyphics on her wide back as she cups his balls with delicacy, exploring this body which has now become hers.

The early evening traffic on the M4 is unusually busy and she almost misses her 6.27 train from Charing Cross. She has told her husband she was away at a day seminar on publishing contracts in north London and can't afford to be late.

She is the first to call the following morning.

No regrets? he asks her.

None at all, she answers.

She is in fact surprised at how little guilt she feels. She never thought it would be so easy.

Again?

Yes.

When?

It's awkward for her to take too many days off from her job without arousing her husband's suspicion at the dwindling of her holiday entitlement. They meet for drinks halfway between their respective offices, find it difficult to keep their hands to themselves and make a frantic beeline for his office where they fuck still half-dressed on the floor.

They manage two meetings a week. She uses every excuse they can concoct for her evening absences from home: sales conferences, drinks with colleagues, meetings with authors from out of town.

They are consumed by each other, travelling on a runaway train of absolute lust and gratification.

Between the fucking, she is quiet, almost reticent to discuss the affair.

Yes, she says to him, the sex is great. Surely, that's enough?

For him, it no longer is. He is the one who has to return to an empty bed and think of her sleeping next to another man who still touches her, makes love to her, shares a life of small nothings, sees her face drowsy when she awakes in the morning, watches her dress, shave her legs, fart, sigh, live. He knows she is only giving him a small part of her and he wants it all.

Initially, he realises, it was lust, something about her that made him vibrate all other, but now he has tasted her, it has turned into something else and he fears telling her this. He's in love. And no longer wishes to share her.

They fuck like rabbits, abandoning all modesty or civilised manners.

She has her period. They fuck. He withdraws his cock from her innards, all coated with blood, dripping come and jam-like matter. He wipes his hand on his red cock and paints the white expanse of her flesh with their combined emissions, outlining her nipples with sharp red circles. The carpet remains stained for months.

He comes inside her once again. She slides away from him and takes his cock, still coated with her own secretions, into her greedy mouth and cleans him.

One evening, he just doesn't know how he has managed to retain his hardness for a fourth fuck in under three hours, and his orgasm courses through him like a bomb exploding, both sheer pain and ecstasy. She is on her knees on the hard office floor, her rump raised, the way she likes it with her husband or previous men, he knows, he collapses on her as he comes. She turns her head back.

Are you OK? she inquires.

Yes, he whispers. I love you.

She doesn't respond.

He disengages from her, withdraws his already limp cock from her gash and lowers his mouth and licks her raw cunt, his tongue sliding inside her and sucking out his own come. It tastes of her. Then he kisses her mouth. They exchange the fluids. She knows what he is doing and does not protest in the slightest.

The more they fuck, the sharper his desire for her becomes.

He turns down any job that might take him away from London if only for a day, in case it's an evening when she can free herself.

They manage a whole week-end together, thanks to a regional book fair in Nottingham. It's the first time they have spent a whole night together. Not that they sleep that much.

They have their first argument.

He binds her hands to a chair while they fool around. She

is immobilised. He positions himself and enters her unexpectedly. She is already soaking wet and soon comes with a blissful scream. She confesses to other fantasies of bondage and submission. He refuses to untie her and fucks her mouth until she chokes and gasps for air.

They stay entwined for hours, the silence between them worth more than a thousand words.

She is on duty at the Frankfurt Book fair and he tags along, spending the nights in her room when she returns from the daily round of parties and receptions. He hates the German town and its invasive greyness and dead buildings and sky. He trawls the red light district during the day. On the second night there, they try anal sex for the first time. Something they've long discussed and fascinates them both. It just happens in the midst of an embrace, there is little resistance and he breaches the wall of her sphincter without undue pressure. Jesus, Jesus. She is wonderfully tight and the heat around his cock feels strangely different. He comes quickly. It felt good for him. There is vain feeling of triumph, and jealousy: something she has never done with her husband. She falls asleep soon after.

They return to London.

She has a holiday booked, arranged long before they met. With her husband.

He attempts to dissuade her from taking it, but she refuses. No way can she justify that.

He is annoyed.

She is annoyed he could even have asked and refuses to tell him where she and her husband are going.

Not New York, I hope? he queries.

No.

He is reassured. He has promised her he will take her there the next year.

She is only away for a week. His curiosity is intense.

He remembers her husband was brought up in Scarborough, on the Yorkshire coast. And that his mother was a bit of an alcoholic, according to her.

He locates the mother and calls her on the phone.

He pretends to be an old university friend of her son who is anxious to get in touch, and learns they are in Ibiza. The woman is garrulous and he conducts a long conversation with her, quizzing her about the marriage and the fact the couple have no children despite all their years together, a sore point over which Kay has always clammed up. She clearly is not enamoured of her daughter-in-law. He is confident the woman will have no memory of their telephone conversation within a few days. He introduced himself under false name anyway.

How was Ibiza? Sunny?

You bastard. How did you find out?

A private dick has his ways.

She just smiles mischievously.

Their routine is now well-established. She phones him every morning at 10.30 after they have both processed their mail. If she cannot free herself in the evening, they share a sandwich over her lunch break in a Soho Italian coffee house. If she can find an alibi, she comes straight to his office; they no longer require the pretext of a hotel bar to meet in before a fuck.

Arm in arm, still wet from their sexual exertions, a mountain of tenderness growing between them, they sit on the floor. It's a colder night, she is wearing his shirt.

So?

So what?

Well, it's nearly three months.

Already?

Happy?

Of course.

So say so…

I'm happy. Satisfied? What else do you want me to say. This juggling isn't easy, you know, one of these days he's going to become suspicious.

Leave him.

What?

You heard me. Leave him. I want you to live with me.

Gee, it's such a big step to take.

I know.

Throwing away seven years just like that.

Listen, Kay, you said the other day I was the best lover you had ever had…

Four other guys and a husband don't make me an expert, you know.

He smiles.

I want you, he says.

You have me, she answers, pointing to her body, she is still leaking.

I want all of you.

Can't you be satisfied with what you have, Martin?

I love you.

The next day, she is attending a sales conference in East-bourne and sharing a room with another female colleague so he is unable to join her. Followed by a week-end. A dinner party she is organising for some friends from her Cambridge college and some City friends of her husband's. Their next assignment is on Monday evening at his office.

Her Monday morning call is late.

When she phones, her voice is cold and remote.

Can we meet at lunch?

Sure. A pleasant extra. But still OK for tonight?

The pub off Charing Cross Road, she suggests.

She walks in on the hour, one of the rare punctual women he has ever known, he reckons.

Why does his heart feel so bad the moment he sees her?

She has had second thoughts, she tells him. She just doesn't want to hurt her husband. He is too dependent on her. The affair is going way too fast. They cannot go on like they have been.

You mean you want it to be over?

He is struck dumb by the pain that races through his soul.

I don't know, she says. Maybe we can stay apart for, say, three months? Not see each other. It will give us both time to reflect, to think about things.

That's a brush off, Kay. You know it, I know it.

No, Martin. Let's just see if we feel the same in three months?

I know I will.

She is annoyed.

Well, I won't know what I feel until then.

He loses all impulse to protest any further. He is aware nothing will sway her determination.

She rises from the seat. She hasn't even touched her drink.

Bye.

He feels sick.

Worthless.

Maybe he knew deep inside the affair could not last forever, but he never thought it would end this way, so suddenly, with no real sense of closure.

He stumbles back to his office in a daze.

In his mind he composes a final letter, a plea, a cry for help, a supplication for a love lost, a last-chance missive.

It takes him two hours to get it right or thereabouts. Lengthy, complex arguments, expressions of devotion, a mature adult acceptance of rejection, a wish to remain friends, shared joyful past memories and all that. In essence, he begs for just one more meeting, one last fuck, the mercy fuck he feels he deserves.

He prints the page out.

Rings her.

Hi.

Oh! You know I don't like you phoning me at work.

I know. I'm sorry.

Is your desk still close to the fax machine?

Yes.

I'm sending you a letter right now. Wanted you to read it immediately. The post wouldn't have reached you until tomorrow.

I see.

He feeds the sheet of paper into the fax machine and punches in the publishing house's number.

It's coming through, she said.

Can I wait while you read it?

I suppose so.

There is a long silence. He hears her coughing.

I see, she says.

I'm begging you, Kay. For the sake of all we had. Please, pretty please.

He can feel her hesitation.

All right, she finally says.

Thank you, he says. Tonight?

No, not tonight. I promised Chris I would be home early. Things we have to talk about.

Tomorrow then?

OK, she replies.

Relief washes over him. And he realises it's a Tuesday.

Usual place and time?

She agrees.

He then asks her if she could wear the clothes she wore for their first Heathrow hotel assignment. The swirling multi-coloured dress, the black bustier, the stockings and the low-heeled ankle-high boots.

The request doesn't surprise her. By now, she's well accustomed to his sentimental touches. But she reminds him that a final evening together is not going to change her decision.

I am sadly aware of that, he answers.

She hangs up.

By the end of the day, he is in the heart of the deepest blue funk. Filled with both sadness and unfathomable anger. He searches his mind for schemes, complicated methods that might lead to her returning to him, but also knows how futile they all are.

He can't think of life without her any more.

It hurts too much.

He's going mad.

Is she going to tell Chris about the affair and the last three months tonight and beg for his forgiveness, save her marriage?

He doubts it, she's too secretive for that, he feels. She will attempt to mend bridges, set the marriage back on the right track, but without giving herself away.

What if her husband found out? Surely, he would never accept it, would throw her out.

He frantically drafts an anonymous letter to the journalist, denouncing her. Can't send it to their flat. Too obvious. His work? Makes a few phone calls and discovers the address of the press agency.

What if he confronts her with it? She'd recognise the printer. For a brief moment, he thinks of cutting every single word or letter out of newspapers and magazines, but realises it would take ages and is just too corny really. Kay would guess he was the sender. She wouldn't forgive him or come back to him under any circumstances if she suspected him of such a vile and under-hand piece of action.

His despair deepens and takes on a darker tone.

If her husband was no longer on the scene, maybe?

A car accident?

Murder?

Could he actually murder a stranger anyway? Well, not quite a stranger, just her husband.

No, he'd become the first suspect.

And lose her a second time.

But the seed has been planted in his mind.

Above all, it's his jealousy for Chris that consumes him, burns all the way down to his guts. It's not that he can't live with the rejection but the fact she has chosen this other man against him. This bastard of a journalist who will continue to enjoy the favour of her eyes, the despoiling of her body, the cushion of her silken flesh, who will hear her say Jesus, Jesus when he accidentally hits a raw nerve when they fuck, who will peer at the squareness of her regal white arse as her intimate apertures beckon, the red rose flower of her cunt, the puckered brown crater of her anus.

The pornographic images drive him halfway to crazy.

No other man deserves her.

His Kay.

His wonderful Kay.

And the nightmare of his imagination rushes onward. He can picture it all: she returns to her husband but eventually gets bored with him again, but out of pride refuses to return to the safe harbour of of his arms and finds another man who pleases her lust, another cock to fuck her, to use her.

No. It's inconceivable. Mustn't happen.

There is a perverse, twisted logic to it. He knows he's not the first jealous man to come up with the equation, but it's no consolation.

If I can't have her, then no one should, he mutters, sinking into a heavy sleep.

It's a rare occasion when she is late but, today of all days, she is. The anxiety dances frantically around the pit of his stomach. He runs through possibilities: she has changed her mind and will after all deprive him of his last, mercy fuck, Chris has forbidden her to come, she can read his mind and knows what he is thinking of doing, something bad has happened to her. The rushing thoughts dance a light fantastic in his brain.

He knows her habit of always using the back stairs when she comes to see him, rather than the front entrance of the building and the lift. Discretion being the better part of valour and her phobia of being seen here by someone who might know her. He had an extra key to the side entrance cut for her two weeks into the affair. So no one will see her entering the building. The way she wanted it.

He hears her long, steady steps in the corridor outside his suite of offices. She knocks.

He takes a deep breath.

Opens the door and lets her in.

Hello.

Hi.

He attempts a peck on her cheek, a peace offering, but she turns her face away. Her eyes are cold, dark steel.

He looks her over.

As he requested, she is wearing the outfit he remembered so well.

She walks past him to the main office and sets her bag down.

He locks the door.

I came, she says.

Thank you, he answers.

I'm sorry it has to end this way, she tells him. But one day you'll agree it's better. Less acrimonious.

I never felt there was any acrimony, he protests.

There would have been, she continues. It was all going too fast, Martin. Getting too serious.

I'm truly sorry. I was just being honest with you about the strength of my feelings.

Yes. And that's what worries me.

Why? he asks her.

She doesn't answer him.

I told Chris all about us yesterday night. Well, that I had been having an affair. I didn't mention your name or who you are, that would have been pointless really.

And?

He was very hurt. But he had his suspicions, you know, all my absences and late evenings. He blames himself, feels he was too obsessed with his own career, neglected me. He was angry, too. Insisted that I tell him who you are.

So what will happen with the two of you?

I've apologised. It was a long night. Neither of us slept at all. He knows I am breaking up with you tonight and is waiting for me at home. I only have an hour or so, Martin. I've promised I will be on the 9.10 train.

He knows?

Just that I'm telling you it's over. He doesn't have to know more.

I understand.

She reaches for the lower button of her bustier.

Let's do it. For old time's sake. Her tone of voice is quite unsentimental and angers him deeply. She wants it to be a cold, passionless fuck.

She continues to undress.

He just stands there waiting and watching as every button is undone, every piece of clothing unzipped, stockings rolled down and her black lacy knickers lowered.

Her beauty overwhelms him.

She is naked.

She looks at him, humourless.

Your turn, she says.

It had often been a running joke between them how much he liked her fully undressed before he shed any of his own clothing. My voyeur, she used to call him.

He drowns in the vision of her nudity.

His heart shatters and flies to every corner of the zodiac.

How do you want me? she asks, still remote and business-like, clearly eager for the whole, now distasteful act of forni-cation to be over.

The condemned man's final wish? He tries to make a joke of it, but she is in no mood for it and remains impassive.

For a few brief seconds, the unacceptable side of his mind imagines her below him and his sharp cock digging deeper inside her than he has ever travelled, literally tearing her apart.

But this is not to be an act of vengeance or vindictiveness, he reminds himself.

On your knees, he orders her.

She turns her back to him and goes down to the carpeted floor.

The bottle of chloroform and the cloth are on his desk, out of her sight.

He places the piece of fabric over the bottle's opening and tips it over. The colourless liquid soon soaks in. He goes over to Kay and places the cloth against her face, smothering her nose and mouth. With his other hand, he holds her down. She doesn't struggle much and her energy quickly ebbs and she falls unconscious, her knees buckling, falling on her side. Her foot catches the edge of the desk and twists. Another bruise in prospect. He remembers how her milky skin marked so easily.

And how the strength of her orgasms would colour her whole front, flushing scarlet, from neck to cleavage. A tell-tale sign of extra-marital sex which sometimes took almost an hour to disappear and had to be taken into account together with her return train schedule from Charing Cross station.

The deed is done, and he knows that now there is no turning back.

No more sentimentality.

He has the medical and the true crime books that were given out to the delegates at the crime writers' conference. He has studied them well over the course of the last twenty-four hours. He pulls the large plastic sheets from their protective wrapping, and lines up the extra large black refuse liners.

Inside his desk drawer are the scalpels and saws.

He knows it's going to be messy.

Already in his mind he is rehearsing the disposal of the remains. He has it all very carefully planned out. A private detective can think laterally, guess how the opposition reasons.

What he is about to do is horrible, he is aware, but it's easier to make body parts disappear. A whole body has a bad tendency to reappear, whether buried, drowned or concealed. And is so much easier to identify.

But Martin knows he will see it through.

It takes him almost two days to cut up Kay's body and another week to scatter the bin liners all over the country, using a judicious combination of building sites, rivers, burial grounds, industrial ovens and sea.

Throughout the whole operation, he forbids himself to even think. He goes through the sad motions like an automaton. The plan works. The hardest part is burning her clothes. In a moment of folly, he even hesitates, thinks of retaining something that will remind him of her, that will still harbour her smell, her lost intimacy, to cover the encroaching images of saw against bone, of scalpel slicing through sinews, of her million curls before he fed them to the flames. But he knows it would be wrong. And dangerous.

So, finally, it's over.

But, as he feared, he can't forget her, and the memories of

their love and his infamy begin to grip his life in a cruel lock of self-loathing and disgust.

The nightmares begin. Invading every corner of his sleepless nights, eternal torture with shades of hell, a film loop he can't stop, unrolling on and on, every variation more painful than the one before, cutting, shredding what's left of his soul.

No one comes asking for her.

He concentrates on his job. Traps another adulterous couple in a Golders Green bed and breakfast and obtains the necessary compromising photograph. He finds a lost dog. Locates a hacker who's playing havoc with a chemical conglomerate's web site. Checks up on the truth and falsities of job applicants for a head hunter.

Life goes on.

He still thinks of Kay.

Every minute of every day, even when his mind is switched off. Sometimes he sheds tears. There is no one he can talk to. Every day is a day in hell.

His mind is wandering. There is a knock on the door.

The name of today's client is Christopher Streetfield.

And a true professional never turns a job down, does he?

11: Martin

What was I expecting? A dark, wet dungeon? The Hollywood version of a brothel with candles smoking and corduroy drapes over the stone walls like flock paper in an Indian restaurant? The House of the Rising Sun (well, this was New Orleans after all), with dusky black maidens barely clothed in white chiffon catering to all the customers' perverse needs with a look of terror and sad acceptance in their eyes?

It was none of that.

It was deceptively normal.

A drawing-room with understated Southern elegance. Well-dressed people sitting in deep armchairs and upholstered leather couches and conversing just above the level of a whisper while sipping tea or coffee from exquisitely fine porcelain cups and saucers balanced on their knees.

Cornelia wore a striking little black dress, its cleavage invaded by the porcelain white of her skin, the velvety material waltzing barely an inch from her nipples, her stockinged legs on full display from mid-thigh down. And a leather collar with sharp silvery metal studs around her long neck. Almost a dog collar, but no dog had ever worn a choker with such poise and calm. The ensemble was completed by a pair of shiny, black low-heeled shoes.

Every man in the room where we sipped drinks in silence only had eyes for her. As her presumed Master, I was an object of dire envy. I wore the black silk suit I only wore for weddings and funerals, made to measure on the occasion of a trip to Bangkok some years back. My shirt, socks, shoes and newly-acquired tie were also black. If not sinister, I reckoned the outfit at least made me seem a bit slimmer than I was.

Some of the other guys were dressed even more formally, tuxedos, dinner jackets and colourful waistcoats, the women alternately garbed in haute couture dresses or, like Cornelia, in understated, demure outfits. At any moment now, I expected someone to bring out the cigars and beckon the women out of the room so that the men present could get on with their smoking and business talk. It was like being parachuted forty years into the past.

So, was this where all the curious strands of the case were meant to unravel?

I had not been idle during the past day. I also owned long lists of phone contacts and I'd sent and received several handfuls of e-mails pursuing the details of Cornelia's identity. It was too dangerous to stay in ignorance. By now, I knew that we were not searching for Louise Poshard for the same reason. Cornelia was danger incarnate. She was not in the business of finding people for the sake of finding them. What I still couldn't puzzle out was why her elder sister would take on my services to find the errant Louise and order a hit on her separately? Or was it just a charade and had Kay's husband ordered my own execution? Still, I had taken a shine to Cornelia and the vibrations coming from her direction did not feel dangerous to me. Nor amorous, I feared. I think I amused her. Which was better than nothing, I supposed.

But I knew I would soon find out

Cornelia and I had been offered tea or coffee by a middle-aged matron who had opened the door to us and confirmed our alleged identity. We had been expected.

'I will lead you to the lounge,' she had said, the accent sounded Texan to me but I was no expert. Once in Omaha, Nebraska, every local had thought I hailed from Australia of all places, so I knew how foolish it was to rely on a person's voice to pinpoint their place of origin. 'We are expecting further guests before we can begin. I do hope you can bear with us,' addressing me and rudely ignoring Cornelia, acting subservient at my side, a most alluring appendage.

A young, seemingly unattached woman in a white cotton smock played an easy listening classical repertoire on the piano in the corner of the large room.

A large, balding man in a perfectly tailored white dinner jacket walked over to us, a thick Cuban cigar in his hand smouldering aromatically. He smiled silently at me and I nodded in recognition. He took this as my agreement to circle the seated Cornelia.

At ease in her role, she modestly lowered her eyes towards the carpeted floor. With his other hand, he slowly touched her, dragging a finger around the curve of her neck. His smile widened approvingly and his fingers moved to her chin. A movement of his wrist and she raised her head and now held his gaze. A finger traced the contour of her lips. Cornelia half-opened her mouth and the finger entered her, both a gentle violation and an assertion of his domination. She sat proudly, sustaining the examination with icy determination. He withdrew. Looked back toward me.

'Well trained?'

'Yes,' I replied.

'I would love to see her put through her paces,' he remarked, drawing on his cigar. 'A most attractive specimen.'

'Yes,' I confirmed.

'Maybe later,' he suggested. 'Let's see how the evening proceeds.' He retreated.

I was about to mumble something in response when a new set of arrivals were chaperoned into the room.

Familiar faces.

Nola Poshard and the man I assumed to be N.

Like me, he was mostly clad in black from head to toe, but

Nola was a veritable picture of menace, her fiery hair catching every ray of light in the room in a halo, her eyes dark and animal, circled by kohl, and her lips the savage red of dark rubies. She wore a pale beige leather dress which perfectly emphasised her lithe frame. Her bare arms were weighed down by heavy silver bracelets and her shining nails were painted dark green. Woman as night predator.

She saw me immediately. If my presence here surprised her, she kept her composure well.

She made a deliberate beeline for us. N followed a pace behind her.

'Mr Jackson...'

'Ms Poshard...'

'Somehow, I didn't expect you'd get this far,' Nola Poshard said to me. 'Welcome to a house of pain.'

'I was given a job. I'm doing it,' I answered.

'Well done,' she said. 'But I've managed to track the little bitch down here through another source, so you may consider your services no longer required, Mr Jackson. My cheque will reach you when you return to London.'

She caught sight of Cornelia in the seat beside mine. Her eyes lit up with both curiosity and sudden envy.

Unless Nola was a better actress than I gave her credit for, it appeared Cornelia wasn't her other source. My initial pet theory was falling down in flames. So, who was Cornelia actually employed by? Was there another player lurking in the dark of this strange game?

'Who is your lovely companion?' Nola asked.

On cue, Cornelia lowered her eyes again.

'Her name is unimportant,' I said.

'How true,' Nola smiled, giving Cornelia a lustful once-over. 'But a very beautiful object nonetheless,' she added.

I winced. Visions of ritual needles piercing Cornelia's parts and the sound of fierce whips breaking the virgin surface of

milky skin and drawing deeply-etched lines of blood in geo-
metrical patterns of infamy.

'Most beautiful.' The basso profundo of N's voice interrupted my brief daydream, as he confirmed Nola's assessment
with a deep, connoisseur-like, sense of appreciation.

'Oh, I haven't introduced you,' Nola said. 'This is N. A
very good friend.'

'We've already met, I think,' I answered.

He raised a bushy eyebrow.

'Although not in ideal circumstances,' I added.

I was now sure he was the man who had searched the
room in Amsterdam and attacked me. Something in his
posture confirmed it. You just have to rely on instinct in this
game.

The lights dimmed.

During the course of my research the previous day, I had
heard a story about this place. It had taken place six years
before when it wasn't called the Moby Lounge and func-
tioned more as a very special kind of brothel. Catering for the
more extreme and depraved tastes of the Louisiana elite and
hedonists. It was thought these events had contributed to the
momentary closure of the establishment and its later reopen-
ing as a more exclusive place of pleasure for a similarly
selective dom/sub clientele.

The story had touched something inside me and I couldn't
erase it from my memory, despite its total lack of connection
with the case at hand.

A young British woman had somehow ended up on the
extreme shores of the Bourbon Street market for sex. She was
on the run, but no one knew from what. A failed marriage, the
police, depression, self-loathing, it could have been anything.
She was ready for anything in this mad dash for oblivion.
Whoredom, drugs, alcohol, she embraced them all avidly.

But even in the depths of her degradation, the endless humiliations she readily submitted herself to in her frantic bid to abolish her past, she held on to her inner beauty somehow. A quiet pride among the dirt and the exploitation of her body and senses. Never did she even shed a tear, even in the worst moments of pain. Which only served as an extra incentive for her users, her torturers, to imagine worse ordeals for her mind and body.

Maybe behind the dead eyes dulled by the beatings and forced sex, there was still a core of hope that sustained her.

They sold tickets to watch her being fucked by the most savage studs and massively endowed black men. She bled, winced but never said a word. The cocks cruelly stretched both her apertures, sometimes more than one at a time as she lay spreadeagled on a dirty mattress on an improvised stage, her hands bound to her side to immobilise her. They ceremonially attached her to wheels and whipped her until she fainted. They auctioned her and watched her gag and choke on the ejaculate of men discharging down her throat and in her mouth and she was forbidden to swallow until it spilled from her parched lips. They filmed her being gang-banged. She never protested. She had no need of money. Just the room upstairs in which she was locked every night following the atrocious festivities. And food.

It's terrible how imagination has no bounds.

With razor blades, they cut thin valleys beneath the mounts of her small breasts and had her copulate with them as the blood dripped downwards and washed over the intricate connection of their cocks and her genitals.

Her silence just served to excite them more.

They erected a wooden cross and bound the English girl to it in a parody of crucifixion and used belts and sticks on her, and obscenely thrust objects into her. They held her there for hours on end, keeping her conscious with judicious cups of water to her lips or sponged against her burning forehead. They snickered when she couldn't avoid urinating and the jet shamefully spurted in an arc from her cunt. One of her torturers caught the stream in a glass and had her drink it. She retched but somehow avoided being sick. They smiled when she could no longer avoid defecating and the shit dangled down from her already well lubricated and open arse, down the wooden plank her back was roped to, and dropped to the floor. They finally untied her and she had lost control of her limbs and fell to the ground, slipping in her own excreta. They shouted at her that she was a dirty slut and pissed on her as she lay on the ground, washing away some of the shit sticking to her white skin before hosing her down properly. She became feverish for days after this ordeal and they took fright and fed her with antibiotics.

But the blonde with the mass of curly hair got better.

So, the next time, they had her mounted by a dog.

They had injected her with a strong tranquilliser before to render her docile. Just in case.

Someone remembered hearing of alleged exhibitions of women with donkeys in Tijuana just after the war and they were nervously contemplating the idea for future entertainment.

By now, the woman spent half the day in a state of docile stupor under the influence of the drugs they were injecting her with.

A man, also a Brit, arrived in town searching for her.

A ghost from her past.

He managed to track her down and, with the help of another whore who worked there and had taken pity on the English girl, bluffed his way in.

He locked himself in a room with her after paying for her services. No one knew what either had said. But he became her angel of salvation. Before anyone realised, he had offered her release from her terrible ordeal and broken her neck. And then hanged himself from the ceiling of the room.

The scandal was hushed up and six months later the place had reopened under a new name.

I asked the man who related this story to me what the names of the man and woman had been, but he didn't know. Not that this revelation would have meant anything to me. They were just two more souls who had been transported by a wave of past failings and misery to the shores of Bourbon, washed up into a world without pity which had no time for the frailties of the business of living.

It all begins to unravel.

In slow motion.

As if in a dream.

In stop motion animation.

Or, like in quiz, all of the above.

Take your pick.

Events in the flickering light of a strobe light. Difficult to fathom, their significance at times obscure, out of reach. Like a puzzle in the process of being assembled but somehow in the wrong order, defying sense and logic.

But then, as you know well, I am the one who is telling you this story.

This is how it happened.

This is how it might have happened.

This is the way I wanted it to happen.

Tick where appropriate.

Remember: I am an unreliable narrator and you have to trust my fallible imagination if events unfurl at which I wasn't even present, where I was not in the same room, could only guess at the words said and unsaid.

So, trust me, I'm a private eye. I can see things you don't see.

The lights in the room dimmed and the runaway train I had been a passenger on this far finally reached its confused destination in its journey through the map of tenderness, the map of human emotions.

In silence, like velvet, a half-dozen women were ushered in. Some were partly nude, others utterly so, all wore tight leather collars around their neck, a symbol of their servitude. They were all young, generally slim, and kept their heads bowed as they were led in and required to stand at attention by the wall.

I recognised Louise immediately. As did Nola, whose breathing just a chair away from me sharpened in its intensity. N purred a cruel sigh of satisfaction.

There could be no doubt about it. Even more so than in the photos I had been provided with, she was like a smaller, kinder version of her sister. The same lips, a similar litheness of body, the way she held her head. The flip side of Nola's dark coin.

All she wore was a bustier, beneath the emblematic collar.

Her genital piercings and jewellery were well in evidence.

'She is beautiful,' Cornelia whispered in my ear, 'in her submissive way.'

I couldn't keep my eyes away from the row of gold rings littering the mound of her cunt.

The young women standing next to her, denied all clothing, also had a ring below, but an inch or so higher than her slit, attached it seems to either her clitoris or its fleshy hood, I couldn't see from where I was sitting. Her dark, elongated nipples were also pierced by rings.

A third girl, she seemed the youngest of the bunch, had been allowed a modest dress, but sported a thick ring dangling from her nose, pierced through her septum, like an animal or the sort of African woman you'd see photos of in *National Geographic* or documentaries. It was horrible, the worst possible humiliation I could imagine.

A nod, and a couple rise from their seats and approach the parade of girls and lead one away to the nearby door she had just made her way through.

Murmurs.

There is no time to confer with Cornelia.

Nola and N are moving towards the exposed Louise as other spectators of the Moby Lounge move from cluster to cluster of attendants, few words exchanged, hands testing flesh, on shoulders and knees, a finger there between a submissive's teeth, her quality being estimated like a piece of meat. Cattle. A skirt being raised ceremonially by an owner to show off his woman's white rump to the appreciation of another dom. I realise it's not only the young slaves who have been made available to others, but there is a free exchange market operating between the couples present. Take your pick.

Cornelia nudges my rib with her elbow and motions me to follow her as she matches her step with Nola and N. I hasten to catch them up.

Louise raises her eyes and a look of dismay races through her features as she recognises her sister and the cruel gaze of the older man who once tortured her.

'So there you are, my sweet,' Nola says, triumphantly, passing her fingers through her sister's lank hair.

Louise remains silent. Slaves are not allowed to speak, it appears. But the fear that chills her is visible to all.

'You have a room where you may be used?' N asks the young woman.

She bows her head dejectedly.

'Let's proceed then,' Nola says. 'I think serious punishment is called for after your untimely escapade.'

'We should like to join the celebration,' Cornelia says.

N tut-tuts.

'Mr Jackson, I am surprised, a slave with opinions? Bad form. Very.'

The five of us are now in the corridor.

Cornelia's face reddens. She realises she has taken a wrong step.

We exchange glances.

'She is sometimes unruly,' I excuse her.

'She should be taught a lesson,' Nola says.

'I shall do so,' I answer.

'Maybe I should?' N suggests.

'Yes,' Nola continues. 'What a good idea. N is a very experienced disciplinarian. He will know how to instil some sense of obedience into your girl, Mr Jackson.'

Cornelia bites her lip.

'You join my sister and I,' Nola says. 'Let N teach your girl some manners. I'm sure there is a room available for them.'

I look Cornelia in the eyes. She imperceptibly lowers her chin. I'm sure she can take care of herself. We part.

Doors. Squares of light in the penumbra of the Moby Lounge's labyrinth of private alcoves.

'So you thought you could just run away, could you, Louise?' Nola says.

A tear pearls down Louise's cheek.

Nola hands me a pair of handcuffs and asks me to secure her sister to a heavy metal bar fixed into the wall. I do so as delicately as I can. Still, the young woman remains silent.

'Kneel,' N orders.

Cornelia obeys.

'I want to fuck your mouth,' he says.

Cornelia advances her hands and skilfully zips open his trousers and pulls his cock out.

He is already hard.

He enters her humid warmth.

I stand watching the two sisters embrace. Mouth devouring mouth, Nola's nails digging sharply against Louise's back, drawing a crossword of thin blood. I imagine tongues lapping, coiling against each other in the dark crevice that joins them.

Nola detaches herself from Louise.

'Yes, I always did enjoy the taste of you,' she says.

She turns to me.

'You like her, don't you, Mr Jackson?'

I am undressed. I had initially protested but Nola had insisted I shed my clothes. My erection is visible. I can't deny that they both awaken my senses.

'Suck him,' she orders Louise.

There is a look of protest in the young woman's eyes.

'Go to her, Jackson.'

I approach the wall where she is chained.

Cornelia is bent over a chair, her black dress raised to her waist. N is now on his ninth stroke of the thin wooden cane he has been using on her ass. The lines on her rump crisscross in a jungle of pink vegetation. He is skilful. The pain spreads with the accuracy of an arrow but she will not mark. With every contact of the cane against the porcelain of her skin, Cornelia shudders.

Her hands are bound behind her back.

She feels helpless.

Finally N ceases.

'I do believe you are not a true sub, my dear,' N whispers softly in her ear, the stale air of his breath wafting across her face. 'Too much control. A real slave would have been in tears by now.'

'Fuck you,' Cornelia says.

N smiles.

Inserts the end of the wooden cane into her anus.

'Bastard,' she mutters.

N brings a Swiss army knife out of his pocket.

The sharp blade flicks open and he pulls it slowly across the raw skin of her backside. He reaches the lower hill of her cheeks and cuts her. Quickly, on both sides.

Cornelia moans.

This will leave marks, she knows. Will hurt like hell every time she sits. The cuts are not deep but their placement is strategically chosen for maximum pain, now and later.

Her teeth mash against each other.

N grasps the hem of the black dress bunched above her waist and cuts across it. The garment parts on either side. She is now more vulnerable than ever.

The knife lingers along her back while N ponders where to hurt her next.

'She says she prefers women to men,' Nola says. 'But she is quite skilful, isn't she, Mr Jackson?'

I refuse to answer.

Nola had pulled me away from Louise's mouth just as I was about to come. Fellatio interruptus.

I stood there, pale, hairy, evidently overweight, my cock now drooping. While Louise was sucking me with all the energy of despair, Nola had moved behind me and wrapped the belt of my own trousers around my neck. Yet another slave on a leash. Another fool for sex.

Louise, on the other hand, has clearly given up, her silence full of acceptance. She knows she has lost. If she was expecting a rescuing knight, I am obviously not he.

Nola is in her element. We cower before her strength, both pitifully naked, embarrassed by our nudity. She has not a single hair out of place in her crown of fire, and looks a few feet taller than she is as she looks over us. Her toys. Our domme. The mistress of ceremony.

The final act beckons.

'So, dear little sister,' she asks, 'where is the damn book?'

'I sold it, ' Louise says.

It's like a blow to my gut.

'There IS a book?' I exclaim.

Never have I misunderstood a case so much, I realise.

'You little bitch!' Nola's hands smash against Louise's cheek. She flinches. Nola continues her assault, frantically attacking her sister. Louise's hands are still immobilised and she can barely protect herself from the blows raining down on her. I try to interpose myself but Nola ragefully kicks me in the shins, and violently pulls on the belt which tightens around my neck. I strive for breath and fall to my knees. Nola kicks me again. Her heel catches one of my ribs. It cracks.

'Who are you, then?' N asks.

Cornelia remains mute.

The blade plays a lingering tango across the nape of her neck as N applies further pressure to the long piece of wood encroaching her innards. He adds a finger and then another, stretching her sphincter muscle to impossible limits.

'Hmm,' N remarks as she still refuses to answer him. 'The gal has guts. So how can I untie that pretty tongue of yours, eh?'

He pulls his fingers out. Distractedly passes them under his nose, enjoying her smell. The wrong end of the cane digs painfully against her depths. Her insides are turning to jelly. More pressure, she knows, and the likely results will prove both more abundant and fragrant. Her face blushes deeply at the thought. Sexual use, she can live with but this sort of pro-longed humiliation is deeply excruciating.

Suddenly, he spanks her ass violently with the open palm of his hand. It stings like hell. The wooden cane is dislodged by the impact and she feels the skin tear across her anal aperture. Cornelia winces.

'Oh dear,' N remarks. 'Haven't we made a bit of a mess of your rear features?'

She pointedly refuses to provide him with the satisfaction of an answer, however obscene.

He slips a hand under her front, cups her slight breasts and twists a nipple.

'But there are still some undeniable beauties at the opposite pole, I guess,' he smirks. 'Shall we explore?'

He pulls the sundered black dress from under her.

'Let's have you the other way up, my dear.'

He rises from the chair and allows Cornelia to roll naked down to the floor. Her shoulder makes uncomfortable contact with the thin carpet. Another bruise. He bends down to reposition her.

'A fuck to remember,' Nola says.

I am on my back. My hands are bound behind my neck, serving as a cushion of sorts.

Louise has manually raised another erection out of me.

Nola has Louise squat over me.

The sight of her fragile body, the marks, the cuts, the servile flesh, the golden rings that catch odd reflections of light, all bring a twist to my heart but I have no control over my cock which looms, hard as rock, to meet her.

Nola holds her by the shoulders and guides her down.

Her labia part, the rings slide against the taut skin of my cock and Louise impales herself on me.

She is very dry. The friction is both intense and painful.

Nola now manoeuvres herself directly behind Louise, also squatting over me, her backside in the crook of my hand, and orchestrates the jerky movements of our fornicating rhythm.

'Who did you sell the book to, Louise?'

Down, her lips open like a flower's jaw and engulf me.

'A dealer in Las Vegas?'

Up, she moves along my shaft, inner secretions coating me in her wake.

'What did you do with the money?'

Down, her ringed mouth of fire devours me.

I see her feeble smile.

'Spent it on a good cause.'

Up, her cunt vacuums me up, pulling the thin envelope of skin clothing my penis into her avid maw.

'You little bitch, you.'

Down, my glans scrapes against her cervix, as she grinds herself against me. I feel as if I'm still growing inside Louise, ready to batter a way into her very womb, reaching new, dangerous depths.

'In that case, sweet sister, you no longer mean anything to me. Maybe it's time to finally part ways…'

Louise closes her eyes.

And yet, I know, she once thought she had loved her.

But it was not for me to say and I just lie there, still fucking her, being fucked by her, and Nola behind pulling those invisible strings.

I also close my eyes. In sheer despair at the turn of events. Would I ever understand how women thought, how hearts turned and swirled? I try to abandon myself to the moment, my whole being reduced to a thrusting cock. In the distance, my orgasm is rising in ever diminishing circles through the layers of my consciousness. I abdicate all control.

Soon, the wave of pleasure is in massive overdrive, a juggernaut speeding down the sharp hill of my senses and about to smash against the shore.

I open my eyes.

The ever-vulgar voyeur in me wants to see my fuck partner's face as I come.

Louise's remain closed, a patina of perspiration coats her
forehead.

Up.

Down.

A rivulet of sweat rolls down the valley of her breasts.

Up. Down.

Her lips part.

My eyes focus on Nola, close behind her.

Her hands are circling Louise's neck.

Up.

Down.

N kneels by Cornelia.

'Pretty decoration,' he says, catching sight of her tattoo.
Her shoulder is in pain. Her backside burns and the cuts
beneath her buttocks itch uncontrollably. She is on her side.
'Nice cunt,' N adds with appreciation.

Cornelia's mouth is dry.

She hates this man with a vengeance.

'Ever been fucked with a knife, my dear? Truly fucked?' he
asks her.

Maybe he wishes to position her better for the next
torture, but he decides to loosen her bound hands. Cornelia
knows this will be her only chance. The moment her hands
are free, and before he can pull them forward and immobilise
her again, she swings her left elbow against his body with all
the energy she can summon. N flinches and falls back a step
or two, Cornelia is on her feet, her dancer's legs unfurling.

She is first to the knife he had dropped on impact.

Without a word, she wields the blade against his throat.

'Ever been fucked by a knife?' she asks the slumping body
of the man, as his eyes glaze and the blood spurts from the
deep opening.

He is dead within a minute.

Two rooms.

Bodies. Entwined. White. Blood.

Nola has tightened the leather belt around her sister's neck and pulls.

Still, we fuck.

I want to call out, but my throat is dry.

We fornicate like automatons.

Up and down Louise slides alongside my cock and Nola increases the pressure.

Louise's face goes red. Her lips part further. Orgasm and asphyxiation combining. Her whole body shivers and triggers my orgasm. I come. Her neck snaps. Her muscles clench wildly in their ultimate spasm and throttle my cock in a vice. The pain is unbearable. I lose consciousness.

12: Martin

The road unfurled like a slow ribbon ahead of us. Cornelia and I alternated at the wheel of the rental Pontiac. One drove, the other slept, affording us a chance to nurse our bruises and pain as we raced along the highways of the South towards Nevada, crossing the monotonous Texas heartlands. We estimated Nola was three hours ahead of us, four or five at the most. She must be doing all the driving and would soon be tiring, we felt.

I assumed N was no longer a problem. When we had hastily changed into new clothes in my hotel room, I had spied the blood across Cornelia's front and knew it wasn't hers. She had kicked in the door to the room where I still lay attached to Louise's dead body. She had revived me and the moment I had opened my eyes, the pain in my genitals hit me. Jeez... just the thought of peeing felt like the ninth circle of hell, let alone the prospect of my next, and awfully distant, erection.

'You're lucky I got there before rigor mortis set in,' Cornelia remarked with a rare of display of bad taste and black humour. 'I would have had to cut you apart.'

'It's not funny,' I protested.

Cornelia's black dress was precariously held together at the neck by a safety pin.

'It's my fault,' she said. 'I shouldn't have left the Glock in my bag. Just felt a handbag would be searched or that a submissive would look unconvincing with a bag.'

'A fucking waste.'

My verbal requiem for Louise Poshard.

'Any idea where Nola has swept off too?'

'Las Vegas, I guess,' I replied.

'How come?' Cornelia queried.

'Louise sold the book to a dealer there, it appears,' I said.

'What book?' Cornelia asked me.

'The Le Carré proof. You didn't know about it?' I asked.

She didn't. I had to explain how the case began. Cornelia's eyes shone strangely as I related the whole story to her. She seemed fascinated. How strange: we both seemed only to be aware of separate elements in the puzzle, and had no clue about the whole picture. Rephrase that: I had no clue.

I cleaned up in the bathroom as Cornelia changed into a pair of my jeans and a blue shirt I was happy to spare. Bathed my genitals in tepid water to ease the nagging pain of Louise's last embrace, wondering whether bruises would show up on a penis.

Cornelia looked good in my clothes, but then she was the sort of woman who would look a treat in or out of anything.

'So, the end of the road?' I remarked.

I had found Louise. The fact that my employer had chosen to kill her ended my involvement in the case, I reckoned, however distasteful the whole farrago had become. All I knew was that I was not about to put in a claim for the final half of my fee. Some would even say I had been an accessory to the murder, though I only felt guilty of cowardice. But then that was nothing new for me. Anyway, the generous advance on expenses covered it already. I still assumed somehow that Cornelia had been hired to cover all possibilities, should my investigation have failed. I was wrong.

'I still have to complete my job,' she said. 'It's far from over. I want that cunt Nola.'

She worked the phone.

Nola had rented a car within an hour of leaving the Moby Lounge. With arrangements to drop it off in Vegas a few days later.

Cornelia asked me if I wanted to tag along. Perversely, I agreed. Nola had to pay for her treatment of Louise. I would be glad to see her get her comeuppance.

'I think there are direct flights from Moisan. We can catch one and be there before her. She has a long drive ahead of her,' I suggested.

'No,' Cornelia replied. 'My Glock won't get past airport security.' She waved the sleek, shiny gun at me, then buried it in her rucksack.

She had a point.

It was a very silent journey. Whenever I had questions for Cornelia, she offered no answers or pretended to be asleep. Several times, she had me relate the story of the book again. It appeared to fascinate her.

Telegraph poles.

Roadside shacks.

Gas stations with fly-infested bars where Cornelia always attracted lusty glances whenever we stocked up on water and potato chips.

More telegraph poles punctuating the flat horizon of fields as far as the eye could see.

Shabby motels advertising their wares and nightly rates in garish pink and mauve neon art deco letters.

We shared a room with two separate beds at the Magnolia Inn somewhere in East Texas. Each of us slumped down onto our respective bed and slept fully-clothed. I was so tired I never even dreamt. But I knew the nightmares would come rushing back at the first opportunity. Now that I was responsible for the deaths of two women.

On the road again and still no conversation to speak of.

Two hours out of Las Vegas and I was sitting in the noisy lounge of a small casino built in the middle of nowhere, an incongruous fabrication dropped into a John Ford desert landscape, for those who couldn't hold out any longer and had to gamble as if their life depended on it, before even reaching the mecca of the Strip. Cornelia was on the phone. A Vegas contact had hacked into the hotel network and located Nola Poshard at the Mirage.

Back in New Orleans, Nola had never heard Cornelia speak, so the ploy was worth trying.

The book would act as a bait.

It was Sunday mid-morning. Nola had booked in barely an hour ago so we assumed, rightly, she had so far been unable to contact the dealer who had acquired the rare proof.

Cornelia pretended to now be its owner and to have heard of Nola's interest in retrieving the item. And to be amenable to worthwhile suggestions.

Hook, line and sinker.

The meeting, Cornelia insisted, had to take place somewhere private, as they both knew of the book's strictly illegal nature. Nola readily agreed. Three pm at the km. 95 crossroads, one hour west of the Hoover Dam.

We had scouted the location earlier as we drove in. It was isolated. You could see for miles around for cars coming and any sign of life, or danger.

We ate. There was a steely determination in Cornelia's eyes. She devoured the jumbo steak meal with studied indifference, wincing every time she moved in her seat. At the motel, early that morning, I had witnessed the deep cuts beneath her buttocks as she showered. She had layered the cuts with gauze, but it shifted with every movement of her legs and the cuts rubbed against the fabric of the jeans.

We drove off.

'I presume you don't have a gun?' Cornelia inquired.

'I'm British. We're not allowed,' I answered.

'Figures.'

'Sorry.'

'You stay in the car, then, if Nola arrives on her own. I'll deal with things my own way. No need for you to get involved further.'

I had more than an inkling of her intentions.

Revenge?

I was still unclear about Cornelia's motivations. What had Nola done to her? Sure, the woman had slaughtered her own sister. But Cornelia had not been present and I knew that ice coursed through her veins and one more death meant nothing to her. Death was her business.

'What if she doesn't come to the rendezvous alone?' I asked.

'Then we'll modify the plan accordingly, shan't we?' Cornelia said. I was far from happy about the 'we'.

The dark Chevy Coupe inched down the road, shimmering in the heat haze. Its approach to the crossroads took forever. The sun shone in full splendour, high above us. Inside our car, I was wet, sweating like a pig. Cornelia had insisted we keep the engine switched off so there was no air-conditioning. She had changed into a thin T-shirt, but her forehead remained resolutely dry. Why is it women don't perspire as we do? She cradled the Glock in her lap.

Nola's car came to a halt on the right-hand side of the road, straddling the crossroads. She appeared to be alone inside the coat-dusted vehicle.

Cornelia opened her door and slithered out of her seat, the gun lodged out of view between her body and the back of her jeans. She crossed the dirt road by which we had parked and came to a halt, a few strides from Nola's Chevrolet. There was deathly silence. Nola finally came in view, her slim silhouette approaching Cornelia.

'You?'

'Yes,' Cornelia confirmed. Nola was outside of my line of

sight and I couldn't see the expression on her face.

'So... the book?'

'There is no book, Miss Poshard. Only me.'

'What the hell do you mean?'

Nola took a step backwards.

Cornelia stood rooted to the same spot, the sun beating fiercely down on her blonde hair and shoulders.

'Louise sold the book.'

'I know that. She told me. In New Orleans.'

Nola was attempting to bluff it out. She had guts.

She caught sight of me sitting in the car.

'You're with him?' she asked Cornelia, nodding in my direction.

'So it appears.'

'He works for me,' Nola shot back. 'Jackson,' she called out, 'you helped me find Louise. There is no need for you to remain involved. Let it be.'

Getting no reaction from me, she faced Cornelia again.

'Who are you?' she asked.

'Just a book collector,' Cornelia answered.

'Stop bullshitting me, woman!'

Nola was seriously losing her cool now.

'It's ironic, isn't it?' Cornelia said with a gentle, understated smile, 'You seek a book. I'd love to get my hands on the book in question. And Louise sold the book to pay for my services.'

Cornelia shifted her legs slightly apart and pulled the gun from her belt.

'You're crazy,' Nola said, retreating, but she had no place to run. She quickly glanced across at me, her eyes expressing a thousand words. But all I could remember was the look of triumph spread across her features as she had choked her own sister.

'Posthumous retribution,' Cornelia said and raised the gun.

The first bullet slammed into Nola's forehead, the back of

her head exploding in a flurry of fiery flowers of blood, bone and brain matter.

That initial bullet probably killed her, but Cornelia pulled the trigger another three times. They all punctured Nola as she fell to the ground.

I held my breath as Cornelia calmly walked back towards our Pontiac. What if the next bullet had my name on it? But she lowered the weapon as she neared me.

'When all is said and done,' Cornelia remarked, 'never mock the virtues of professionalism.'

'That's it then?' I queried, the bile rising at the back of my throat out of relief, fear and disgust.

'Yes.'

Cornelia moved into her seat.

'Time to go home,' she said.

We returned the car to the Avis depot at Las Vegas airport. We had thoroughly wiped it of prints beforehand. The Glock had been dumped in the desert, miles from the deadly crossroads. Cornelia was thorough.

Again we shared a room at one of airport hotels and both showered all the dirt and the sweat away in silence, Cornelia moving naked, in all innocence and splendour, between bedroom and bathroom, unworried about my presence. Never, I knew, would I see so much of a woman's intimacy and never even touch her.

Sitting in the departure lounge, waiting for our respective flights to New York and London, Cornelia opened up for the first time.

'It's been a mess,' she admitted, slowly sipping from a tall glass of iced tea.

'You're telling me. So, any plans?' I asked her.

'Yes. Time for a sabbatical. A leave of absence from the killing business. I'm tired.'

'So am I,' I said. 'Very.'

They called our flights.

Cornelia surprised me with a peck on the cheek.

'Goodbye, Martin.'

'The first time you've actually said my name,' I pointed out.

'Really?'

Cornelia smiled, turned away from me and took her customary long strides down the concourse.

Last night, the nightmares returned.

The carnival of female bodies, skin like silk, danced across my night, with the softness of cream, lips, breasts, wondrous curves in all the shapes of heaven, my heart floating across the loneliness, and somewhere, beyond reach, a strange feeling called hope.

Love.

Its tyranny.

The reason we live, and invariably fail.

The reason I killed Kay.

Lust, its contagion.

The reason I remain alive and face every new day with fear.

The reason I allowed Louise's obscene death.

Visions of beautiful bodies destroyed forever, flesh turning to maggots and dust and their pleading eyes in the surrounding darkness screaming at me, every sound a dagger cutting me open, shredding my own flesh into slivers of free fall agony. Essence of self-loathing. Then the screen tears and I awaken, alone at three in the morning in an empty bed in a North London flat, with just the memories. That will never leave me. Another day beckons, things to do, the business of living to keep my mind occupied until sleep comes again and, with it, the procession of horrors, the fruits of my betrayal.

I remain.

And my debt to the dead remains.

So, I shall get up and shave in the morning. Comb my hair and pull tufts of greying strands from the brush. Clean my glasses. Dress in combinations of blue, black and grey. Take the Northern Line to Tottenham Court Road and walk down New Oxford Street to my office in Holborn. Where I shall sit at my desk and accept cases. Industrial espionage, adultery, missing dogs and cats, petty theft. The loneliness tears at me.

It's my first day back following the Poshard case.

There's a message from Joan. She returns to work tomorrow. Hopes I'm well. Anything interesting been happening?

I process the snail mail and the e-mails. A few invoices, one or two possible jobs and tons of publicity leaflets and letters asking me to invest the money I don't have in every possible combination of trusts, shares, government bonds and other get-rich-quick schemes. By midday, the administration has moved from in-tray to out-tray.

There are seventeen messages on the ansaphone.

I click and listen.

Mostly enquiries. Nervous voices who don't know what a private detective might sound like. Some have left numbers. Others will call back. One stationery salesman and a double-glazing cold call. And, three days ago – I was still driving across Texas with Cornelia – Christopher Streetfield, his voice a whisper, asking how I'm getting on, any sign of Kay? Anywhere?

I phone him back at the press agency where he works. To admit defeat and suggest a refund. What else?

A woman picks up the phone on his direct line. Asks me who I am.

A friend, I say.

Streetfield committed suicide, she is so sorry to inform me. His wife had left him, you see. Hanged himself. Left an explanatory note.

I put the phone down.

My third murder.

But life goes on. With the right mental training you learn to take anything in your stride.

I find the mobile number Aida left me in Amsterdam.

Maybe she hasn't yet found Mr ight or Mr Rich or Mr Pimp? I could ask her to fly to London. Bring her child along. Sort of adopt them both. Something in her touches me. Her green eyes, her shy smile, the hurt buried within. I can't offer her much, I know, but maybe we can make a go of it. For a time, anyway. I know I'm more Mr Wrong than Mr Right. Don't know how I will adapt to a woman with a child fathered by another man. I'm too old for her, quite unprepared to start a new family. But I know I'd be convenient for her, provide her and her son with a roof above their heads, some security, maybe a passport. Eastern European women are practical by necessity. And one day she would inevitably meet someone younger or wealthier and leave.

I'm a realist: I know Aida is wrong. Too young. Too this. Too that. That her leaving me is inevitable. But, for now, she's all I have.

That's fine with me.

It would be nice to wake in the morning with the warm softness of Aida's body next to me. While it lasts. She might not banish the nightmares, but maybe her presence will deaden their implacable roar.

Unless they catch up with me and that knock on the door in the morning when I least expect it will be grey men with badges and questions about Kay.

And when they question me, I will not be evasive or a coward any longer.

I will at last confess to the murder of the only woman I have ever loved.

In the meantime, I continue living in a world full of women. I tap out the dialling-code for Holland.

The Do-Not Press
Fiercely Independent Publishing

Keep in touch with what's happening at the cutting edge of independent British publishing.

Simply send your name and address to:
The Do-Not Press (Dept. OTE)
PO Box 4215, London
SE23 2QD
or email us: thedonotpress@zoo.co.uk

There is no obligation to purchase
(although we'd certainly like you to!)
and no salesman will call.

Visit our regularly-updated web site:
http://www.thedonotpress.co.uk

Mail Order
All our titles are available from good bookshops, or (in case of difficulty) direct from The Do-Not Press at the address above. There is no charge for post and packing.
(NB: A postman may call.)